Sigh

SUITED FOR SIN: BOOK TWO

ANGEL PAYNE

This book is an original publication of Waterhouse Press.

This is a work of fiction. Names, characters, places, and incidents either are the product of the author's imagination or are used fictitiously, and any resemblance to actual persons, living or dead, business establishments, events, or locales is entirely coincidental. The publisher does not assume any responsibility for third-party websites or their content.

Copyright © 2018 Waterhouse Press, LLC
Cover Design by Waterhouse Press, LLC
Cover Photographs: Shutterstock

All Rights Reserved.
No part of this book may be reproduced, scanned, or distributed in any printed or electronic format without permission. Please do not participate in or encourage piracy of copyrighted materials in violation of the author's rights. Purchase only authorized editions.

Paperback ISBN: 978-1-64263-114-2

SUITED FOR SIN: BOOK TWO

ANGEL PAYNE

WATERHOUSE PRESS

As always...for my amazing Thomas.
You believe in me more than I believe in
myself...and bring me so many sighs,
each and every day. Thank you for our life
together. I love you.

CHAPTER ONE

It was the day Mark Moore both dreaded and treasured. Every year, he thought the feelings would wane a little.

Every year, he was wrong.

As morning dawned over Nassau, he stood on Cable Beach and watched the sun burn away the early-morning mist and then throw specks of warm gold onto the waters of Delaport Bay. The majority of Nassau still slept, including the fifty men and women from Global Restoration Incorporated he'd be training during the next ten days. In a month, they'd all be needed in Iraq to start rebuilding a school and hospital. GRI thought their training for hell would "take" better in a place that felt like heaven.

The setting didn't help his soul this morning.

He'd accepted the project eagerly enough, knowing damn well over which date it would fall. But since stepping away from the chaos of being a US senator, Mark came to enjoy these training gigs as a pleasant, even welcome, time fill. They gobbled up the lonely stretches between the advisory meetings he still got called to on Capitol Hill and the frequent trips to cheer on Dasha, pop-star daughter extraordinaire, who'd just finished the most successful year yet of her career. So effectively, there was always someplace to be, something to do, enough on the calendar so he'd forget today was on its way. And if he couldn't forget, then maybe he'd be too exhausted to ache. Too weary to grieve. Strong enough not to miss her.

Fool.

"Happy anniversary, sweetie." He murmured it into the balmy breeze, a mocking contrast to the freezing landscape of his spirit. Dangling from his fingers was a collar, white leather encrusted with sapphires, which had been custom fitted for the woman who once wore it. The delicate circle had been empty now for four years. Cancer had severed their mortal time together, but in the depths of his heart, it was as if Heather still knelt before him, submissive and breathtaking. She'd shared his life, borne his child, captured his soul...and yes, worn his collar with all the joy and love in her boundless heart.

There would be no other like her. Mark hadn't even tried looking. God didn't duplicate stars or snowflakes. He sure as hell hadn't duplicated Heather.

"I miss you, my love."

Soft but sure, a voice swirled around his senses like the mist off the waves. He inhaled, letting her whisper fill him, ease him.

As I miss you, Master.

The endearment brought a bittersweet smile to his lips. He braced his feet in the sand, digging his hands into the pockets of his khaki shorts. Despite the peace she brought to his soul, the damn sting behind his eyes got stronger. He gritted his teeth against the invasion. The effort was an abysmal failure.

"Fuck."

When did this get any easier? When did the pain stop?

It won't stop hurting until you stop pulling crap like this. Until you stop revisiting everything.

He dragged in a sigh. It was like inhaling glass. "I know, all right? Damn it, I know."

Mark...it's time to let go.

A harsh chuff burst out. "Topping from the bottom yet

again, love? You know how much that pisses me off."

I'm right this time. You're ready. It's time to move on, to have joy, to live...and yes, to love again. You have so much to give somebody. Go find her. Go guide her. Give her what she needs. Give her all the magic of you. All the magic that I'll always love...

With another whisper of the morning wind, she was gone. For good.

He supposed his system remembered to breathe. For a long minute, he didn't care. The loss ripped through him anew, slashing just as much as the day he'd first laid her in the ground. He stared at the waves, hating them for pretending to roll in at the shore as if nothing had happened, as if his world hadn't shattered all over again. But then the sun crested over the water, blinding in its intensity, shaking him. Oh yeah, as if Heather stood here doing the exact same thing.

It was a new day. It was time to wake up. To continue living. Somehow, he had to. He would. It was going to be hell, but he would.

Two hours later, after showering and changing out of his beach clothes, he made his way to the classroom the resort had reserved for the training. By now his morose mood was jammed down behind the composed, commanding statesman for which GRI had paid a prince's ransom.

The persona wasn't an act. He liked himself in this form, especially today when he brought out a little more of the Dominant in him, in honor of Heather. He looked the part as well. The deep-brown, open-necked shirt matched his eyes. The tan pants were tailored for him, purchased last week when

Dasha had taken him on a father-daughter shopping spree in Chicago, and were half a shade darker than his close-cropped hair, beard, and mustache. He'd been in the city for the GRI briefing and Dasha for a special TV taping. She'd convinced him to let out his "inner rebel" by pairing the whole thing with a new pair of dark-brown boots in soft Italian leather.

His trainees began to file into the room. The crowd, ranging in age from twenty-eight to thirty-five, contained executives and engineers of both genders. They'd all been with GRI for at least a year and had completed a rigorous internal application process to be selected for this task force. The company had put them through six weeks of something close to corporate boot camp, including intense behavioral simulations, days of scheduled *and* surprise physical endurance tests, and countless evaluations to gauge their mental adaptability, including two rounds of planned sleep deprivation. They were the final fifty, gleaned from a field of over five hundred, so the general air of cocky celebration in the room was both tangible and understandable.

It also explained why he couldn't help the comparisons to a high school homeroom. The usual suspects emerged all by themselves. There was the class clown, making himself obvious by the open smirk he flashed upon entering and then turning to his buddies to get off a couple more jokes before they settled in. There was the Barbie and Ken couple, likely to be bumping plastic bodies before today turned into tomorrow. It went on with a few more. He tagged the jock, the drama queen, the fashionista—

And then the one who'd clearly walked into the wrong room.

Mark stopped collating his course packets to watch her.

Though she wore a light knit dress and matching jacket, the business-casual attire matched by a number of women in the room, she might as well have been in a Victorian day gown as she moved, fluid and graceful, down the tiers of the classroom. Despite her smooth bearing, she couldn't completely hide the gentle curve of her hips, hugged by the dress, or her round and plentiful cleavage, kissed by the bottom of her ponytail. That rope of luxurious russet was softened by little tendrils that framed her face, centered by eyes so huge he already noted their color. Deep velvet brown. Her mouth, straight out of an antique cameo, was set with firm concentration. But he noticed a tentative tremor to it as she lifted it in a smile toward him, planting herself in a seat at the front of the room.

That smile. When was the last time anyone had looked at him like that? Without complication. Without expectation. Without anything but a little curiosity and a lot of friendliness.

She *had* to be in the wrong place.

Mark approached, hoping his face gave the same first impression as hers. For the first time in a long time, he wasn't completely confident of himself. "Hello."

She tilted her head, and again it seemed like a Canterbury bonnet belonged there. "Good morning, Senator Moore."

He chuckled. "Hmm. That answered my first question about you."

Her cheeks went the color of two English roses, ensuring he couldn't rip his gaze from her. "What question was that?"

"I was sure you'd wandered into the wrong meeting room."

Her face tightened. Determination swirled in her boundless eyes. "Oh, I'm in the right place. I can assure you of that."

Mark didn't shirk from the intensity of her statement. For

a second, that appeared to stun her. He smiled again, watching every nuance of her reaction to him. And hell yes, he liked that he got to observe it from where he stood. Because she'd chosen the front row of the room, he now stood above her, making her turn that elegant face fully up to him. If he took half a step closer, he'd be able to reach down and take her chin in his fingers, compelling her to arch her head back, exposing more of her creamy neck to him, her eyes closing in willing surrender...

Something flared in his blood. Something hot, unfamiliar, unsettling. Dangerous.

Which was why, like a complete fucking fool, he craved more.

"I can see that now." He indulged that step toward her but shoved his hands into his pockets. Time for a safer subject: the observation that was as clear as the classic nose on her face. "You really want to be here, don't you?"

A pulse jumped in her throat, mesmerizing him. As he pressed on the word *want*, she sent a swallow down that smooth column too. He endured a similar clutch in his own breath. Hell. This wasn't anything he'd felt since—

No. He wouldn't go there. This wasn't going to happen today. *Not today.*

To his relief, she crunched a little frown at him. "We all want to be here, Senator."

"I think you know what I mean." He pulled back a little. But hell, that just made her more breathtaking. Every emotion played itself so honestly across her face. After forcing down a breath, he continued, "Most people applied for this project because of the extra money, the prestige of the deal, or both. And I imagine most think the toughest part of the process is behind them. I'm here to shake those perceptions a bit. Maybe more than a bit." He looked back at her again, letting her see his open assessment. "I won't be shaking you up, will I?"

Her lips lifted in a full smile this time. "No, sir."

She could've told him to fuck off and caused him less shock. He masked the reaction by pretending to clear his throat. Her voice, still so soft and sure, turned the heat in his blood to more than a minor irritation. It took a simple mental click to imagine her *no* getting replaced with a *yes*. As for the *sir*...

It was the first time he'd ever imagined the words coming from someone other than Heather.

Who was she?

"So. What's your name, Ms. I-Can't-Be-Shaken?"

"Rosalind Fabian, sir. I...I mean Senator."

He feigned another throat clearing. "*Sir* is just fine if you're comfortable with it, my dear."

She laughed. The sound was like the rest of her, a rich braid of soft and strong. "And most people call me Rose, if you're comfortable with that."

"Fine, then. Nice to meet you, Rose."

He'd meant to keep it professional. Instead his voice dipped into a range he didn't recognize from himself, borrowing from the thick velvet of her eyes—which now widened a little as his hand fit against hers. Her grip was firm though. And *that* troubled him. He didn't want her so steady when he was near. He wanted to keep her hand locked in his, just before he turned it over by the wrist and pressed his mouth into her palm. He wondered what that would do to Miss Rose Fabian and her composure. She'd erected her personal barricade so painstakingly, to the point that he knew one thing with certainty: it was there as much to keep her from breaking out as others from busting in. But why? What would a kiss like that unleash in her? From her?

Before his mind took that fantasy into risky territory, he released her and backed away. No. Forget risky. The word was *lethal*. He wanted to do things to Rose Fabian he hadn't *thought* of in four years. He wanted more of those eyes that enwrapped him, the smile that unglued him...

And the circumstances that were impossible.

She was a student, damn it. And on her way to Baghdad in two weeks. And at least a decade younger than him.

Yep. *Lethal* said it perfectly.

CHAPTER TWO

She'd gone and screwed it up again. Whatever "it" was.

Rose tried to get in at least one steady breath as the conclusion attacked for the hundredth time in the last three days. It sounded silly, junior high, and ridiculous—but was the only explanation for why Senator Moore had all but ignored her since they'd first met.

Clearly she'd imagined the electricity of their first handclasp. The connection she'd felt from his attention, his hold, his unblinking tawny eyes... It had all been a fabrication. A product of *her* pathetic desperation.

And why not? It made sense. When was the last time anybody had touched her? Her parched libido simply craved sustenance, and now it was jumping to embarrassing conclusions. With a gorgeous, commanding, fascinating... altogether inappropriate man.

He was at least ten years older. An ex-senator. The father of a world-renowned pop star. Living in a world she could hardly comprehend...

He was also exactly what filled her mind in every free moment it had.

So now she had a new mission.

No more free moments.

Even if that meant overcompensating a little. Like participating in every single class discussion. Asking the correct questions. Continuing to sit in the front of the room, determined to prove how much she wanted this...how badly she needed this new chapter in her life.

Needed to slam shut, and then glue down forever, the last chapter.

Not that Mother and Shane were ready to do the same. Like prizefighters grieving a lost title, her mother and brother held up her failure every chance they could. Worst thing was, she kept letting them. In a perverse way, she understood every note of pain behind their glib commentary.

Mother's was always preceded by her traditional sigh. *"We should have seen it coming, I suppose. Owen didn't even have a bachelor party. We all thought he was just being a good fiancé. He was so sweet and respectful."*

Shane just went straight for his male model head tilt. *"Agreed in full, Mother. It just wasn't a good fit. Men like him need a certain type of woman...the right look, the right temperament. You do have moments, Rose, of rather intense emotion. It was best he saw it and nixed everything before you two actually said the vows."*

She'd let it all pass, but now it'd been a year. She was ready to sell the dress, bury the shame, and start the journey toward something meaningful in her life besides wallowing in her shame—so when GRI had landed the contract for the rebuild in Iraq and solicited internal candidates first, she'd gone for it. Had swallowed her nervousness, deciding a degree in environmental engineering might not be the "useless paper" Shane had always asserted. She'd applied, not telling anyone about it. When she passed the intake process and security clearance, it was too easy to continue the trend of silence.

She probably could've kept up the ruse, since Mother and Shane weren't interested in the particulars of her "amusing job," but when the invitations for Chicago's spring gala season rolled in, the gig was up. How did she explain she'd be six thousand miles away instead? She'd gone at them with a determined approach. They could all make a decision that her empty ring finger didn't bode eternal doom for the family. Here was a chance to do something good for the world beyond the tennis club, the polo team, and months of fund-raisers for causes they only pretended to care about. This was a chance to move on. Didn't they all want that?

Apparently not.

She'd gotten Mother's sigh in triplicate first. *"You're going to embarrass us even worse by running away?"*

Shane had tossed aside the head tilt in favor of a full glower. *"Rose, really. It's been barely a year. We're only now getting invitations again to the events that matter. Don't you understand? We need this season to gain face again! How are we supposed to show ourselves in society and explain that you've run off to a desert hellhole for your eat-pray-love break? Couldn't you have chosen Paris, New York, even India?"*

She gripped her pen harder to stop her hand from shaking. "Thoughts on the now," she whispered to herself. Time to stop thinking about events she couldn't undo, about the person she wasn't capable of being. About mistakes that weren't yet forgiven, much less forgotten.

She focused again on the paper in front of her. It was their last session of the day. The senator had instructed them to write down their reasons for initially applying to the team and how those motives had changed by this point, if at all. He'd given them fifteen minutes to consider their answers, urging them to "dig beneath surface responses." She'd filled her paper in about five minutes but took the next ten to stress over every line. Moore had said there were no right or wrong responses, *not* a simple concept for her to understand.

But nothing was easier once she looked up, either.

The man himself fixed a steady, leonine stare on her...not faltering even when their gazes tangled. In response, what did *she* do? Squirmed in silence like a damn idiot, of course—but what was a "normal" answer when one felt as if their answers were already being read by telepathy?

Moore's lips quirked. The look was almost a smile. Millimeters at a time, Rose felt her mouth shifting the same direction.

Ohhhh, hell.

Parched libido, meet beautiful oasis.

He entranced her all over again, making the whole room go away with his intensity. She'd thought of electricity when they'd first met. The same current arced again—only this time, it bypassed the rest of her body, shooting to her most intimate core. Her eyebrows jumped as the arousal spread, making her thighs tingle, sending its stunning impact down to her toes.

That was the instant before the senator's head finally snapped up. He gazed away, his mouth pressing to a firm line. It was a very Capitol Hill look—reminding her exactly who he was. *Senator* Mark Moore. Okay, one who'd stepped down from office six months ago, but still a man who'd bear the title the rest of his life.

And she'd just gawked at him like a teenager mooning at her hunky science teacher.

Hell. Would she ever get something right in her life again?

Best not to consider that answer too hard.

"Pens up."

His voice carried the edge of experience yet the confidence

of command. The rest of the class raised their heads along with their pens, but Rose didn't join them. That tone of his, clipped and commanding, finished what his gaze had started in her sex. Now she contended with drips down her labia and a flush to her whole face. She hoped the writing exercise had been just that, an exercise, and that they wouldn't be actually asked to share what they'd written with everyone. She wasn't sure what her voice would sound like, with her body raging in this condition.

"Who'd like to share their answer first?"

For the first time in three days, she didn't volunteer for the duty. But her die had been cast. From two rows behind her, a snicker broke out. "Why don't we let Rose have the honor? After all, when a woman begs enough..."

Forget the flush. Her face burned now. It wasn't the first time Ryan Johnson zinged a one-liner at her expense. He did it enough back at the office in Chicago, seeming to think his continued friendship with Owen gave him the right. Though Owen had left GRI for the corner office at his dad's firm long before the wedding day, Ryan kept the strings tied nice and tight between them. Turned out that a flawless face and a ripped torso really could get a cheap gutter snake invited to the best parties.

"In your dreams, Ry-Ry," she managed to snap back. It wasn't her best effort, but she usually didn't have to process Ryan's crap with her shields down, her body on fire, and her logic shot to hell. She couldn't summon even a decent eye roll to finish it off.

There was also the matter of him being right. She'd made an idiot of herself, hadn't she? In longing to earn Moore's approval signature on her training docs, she'd instead exposed her true colors, something in a hue between desperate and seriously messed up. Moore would likely make it worse right now too. She could already hear him dressing Ryan down, telling the ass to apologize. Then she'd have to endure Ryan's insincere compliance. And she sure as hell could feel what she'd want to do after that. She gazed at the floor, wondering how hard she'd have to fall to blend into the carpet.

"That's a considerate gesture, Mr. Johnson." Moore's voice now sounded like an ironic tease. "As a reward for such, why don't you take the honor of first stab instead?"

Ryan's two buddies, Kai Thomas and Peter Ferne, chuckled and elbowed him. The three had nothing in common physically, which balanced the fact that they shared the same brain, clearly set on adolescence as the default under tension like this.

Despite their ribbing, Ryan replied, "Sure thing, Senator. I'm game. You want my full essay or just the flyover?"

Rose heard Moore's measured exhalation. "The main points will be fine."

"That's good, because I really have just one."

"And that is?"

"Excellence, plain and simple. I stand proudly for it."

Peter snickered. "They don't call him the human tripod for nothing."

Rose got in her eye roll, if only to herself. "Or the money burner. Or Mr. Atlantic City." She was confident the comment went unnoticed in the round of chuckles that answered Pete's quip. Still, the senator's next sigh had a knowing weight to it.

"Decent start, Mr. Johnson. Maybe a little more detail *is* in order."

"No problem." Ryan shuffled in his notebook. "All right, we all know GRI wasn't the first contractor of choice on this gig. Instead, they selected Renovera. Granted, the big *R* is Swiss and neutral, but they also don't know how to do things properly. They used shoddy materials on the initial build-out and were likely too lazy or just too ignorant to double-check the geo study numbers after pouring the foundation. Now look what's happened. The school is falling down after a year. The hospital isn't even finished. We stand for excellence, for doing things perfect the *first* time. We gotta be diligent, and that's what we're gonna do. I can't wait to get over there and show these bozos how great American companies kick ass the right way."

The class erupted in applause and a round of woots. Everyone except for Senator Moore.

"Not a bad response," the man said after the clapping abated. "And not a bad way to think either. Back in my marine days, I'd have been proud to have you on my team, Mr. Johnson. But"—he paused, letting Ryan have a good preen first—"it comes close to a deadly way to think when you're in a civilian-contracting situation. You're not just representing America and GRI. You're there to absorb and respect the Iraqis in *their* land. You're a visitor, not an invader. Don't forget it. Take the GI Joe attitude into subjects beyond your immediate expertise, such as their food, their drink, their women or, God help you, their religion, and you'll find yourself in a prison with medieval standards at best. Your kick-ass company won't be able to get to you, and your so-called native hosts will use that third leg of yours as your cell torch."

Ryan, Pete, and Kai gave up discomfited laughs. The rest of the class gasped. Rose felt sacrilegious for her gloating smile and tried to hide it. But Moore was back to his homing-beacon stare on her face. She glanced up to find him flashing a secret grin back at her. It had her bracing for his next words. Oh yeah, he definitely had the laser trained on her now.

"Can I go next?"

She secretly hugged Aria Cyrre for the injection. The blonde logistics specialist from the Austin office, who looked like Tinker Bell but could cuss like a truck driver, spoke up from the middle of the room.

"You're up," Moore conceded to her.

"I might be stating the obvious, but this is a chance to be part of history, you know? Taking down that asshole's regime was just the start. We helped make that blood-and-piss mess. I think it's only right that we help clean it up."

As the room broke into chuckles, Moore stepped out from the podium. "Excellent point, Aria. It helps speak to a larger issue here too. Listen up on this, people. It's great to feel good about what you're doing on this project, but the people you're doing it for will not all embrace you as heroes. You *will* meet many natives who see you as part of the boots who kicked the hornet's nest. You're not going to get the Lifetime-TV ending with them, even after those buildings are finished the right way."

He shifted again, hitching a thigh onto the desk next to her. Though Rose ordered herself against it, she found her gaze looking at that leg through the curtain of her lashes. Toned. Marine-hard. *Well, hell.*

He leaned his elbow to his knee. She swore she could feel the heat of his renewed stare. Her heartbeat became a torment again.

"Now we'll have the honor of hearing from Ms. Fabian."

For a wild instant, she contemplated fabricating a reply instead of going with the sappy words on the page in front of her.

But when she lifted her head and confronted the full strength of the man's regard, she faced one unflinching realization.

She'd never be able to give Mark Moore anything less than the truth.

"I think people deserve second chances," she stated. He hardly reacted to that, except for the tiny creases at the tops of his cheeks, which deepened a little. It seemed a good thing. She hurried on. "I really think they deserve it more when their circumstances weren't their direct doing but the world has perceived them to be. These people only want what we all want. They want to walk down the street in peace, to raise healthy children, to have love, to be happy. To help them have that chance..." She shrugged, feeling a little embarrassed now, but finished. "It feels like a second chance for me too."

She didn't know whether the following silence was a good or bad thing, especially because it seemed to radiate from Moore himself. He returned to his feet, but his stance wasn't anything she'd seen in the last two days. His arms, straight at his sides, ended in fists. He looked like invisible tethers held him back—but from doing what? A peek at his face didn't give her the answer. His gaze now looked like a copper mine on fire. His pulse jumped beneath his trimmed beard.

Everything about him made her think of kissing him.

No. Letting *him* kiss *her.* Hard, heavy, brutally.

She almost thanked Ryan for breaking into her thoughts with his newest chortle. Almost.

"Oh hey, Rose. Sorry. I'm not laughing because— Well, I mean no disrespect." She heard his clothes rustling as he swung his gaze around the room. "I think it's...umm...brave of you to share your issues with everyone like this."

The dig couldn't have been more obvious. There was

substance behind the comment, since Ryan had been sitting in the church the day of Owen's famous no-show, but she decided to call the man on his own bluff. Ryan was a conceited coattail grabber but not a cruel prick. "My *issues*, Ryan?" She pivoted in her seat, making sure their gazes met. "You're deciding to bump your project bonus more by applying for group shrink too?"

The guy's surfing-god looks played to his advantage. He shrugged with a disarming smile. "I'm just saying it's not a sin to use work as therapy. It's how half the great corporations of the world got started."

She rolled her eyes. Ryan didn't flinch. The moment begged her to let his taunt lie and walk away. But if she couldn't hold her own even with Ryan, what would the senator think about her ability to handle the rigors of what they'd face in Iraq?

"I'd suggest you heed Senator Moore's advice, Mr. Johnson. Don't tread in areas where you don't have expertise, which, in this case, includes my head."

She swung forward again. Then made the mistake of taking a breath and thinking she could relax again.

"It's nothing to be ashamed of, Rose. You're not the first person to get stood up on your wedding day."

Correction. Ryan really could be that big a prick.

His truth dug in like a murder knife, cold and unhesitating—and accurate. He got her heart right down the middle. She'd come here to put the past away, to start on the clean slate of hope, but that was too damn impossible. Maybe fate didn't use erasable chalk for someone like her. Maybe there would just always be shits like Ryan to throw the board back in her face, making her confront the humiliation all over again. Maybe she should have never made this lame attempt at hope or believed fresh starts could really happen.

She stayed upright as Kai and Pete added their chuckles to Ryan's. But that made everyone else think she was in on the jab, and it was okay to join in the amusement. She deepened her stare at the carpet. The tropical print seemed a better escape route by the second. But damn it, a pair of Cavalli-clad feet got in her way. Not just any feet either. Mark Moore's feet. That single factor made this embarrassment worse than the others. She wouldn't be able to look him in the eye again. No more secret, selfish drags of his warm strength. Not after he knew about her grand failure.

The conclusion, so horrible and final, was what drove her to her feet. And right up the stairs. And right out of the room. Her inadequacy had screwed things up. Again.

CHAPTER THREE

She'd disappeared out the door before Mark trusted himself to push past his fury and speak. Even then the words left him with savage force, cutting through the laughter they'd given Rose as a send-off.

"I think we're done for the day, children. I suggest you use your free time to do something constructive. Like growing the fuck up."

They went silent. It was paltry relief for the protective fire roaring through his body. He let the heat take over and ignite his muscles, propelling him up the stairs two at a time.

Out in the hall, he beheld an empty corridor, a glass wall, and the patio beyond that. Bright hibiscus and lush palms swung lazily in the island breeze, mocking him with their peaceful perfection.

He bit back an oath. She'd bolted fast but couldn't have gone that far. He closed his eyes, drawing on instincts honed on the frontlines in desert shitholes, shutting down his reliance on a visual. He listened instead. And breathed. And hoped she'd give herself away with the patter of fleeing footsteps, maybe the lingering wisp of her fragrance on the air. In the last forty-eight hours, he'd tried like hell not to notice how she smelled. Now he was glad he'd failed. A hint of magnolia, a kiss of vanilla, and a lot of clean, creamy skin...

There it was. Off to the right. Her footfall, frantic and hard, confirmed his conclusion.

Without a second thought, he followed.

The corridor hooked to the left before becoming a flagstone pathway leading through gardens, grottos, and water features. Mark followed it past a koi pond and a gazebo, finally finding her stopped against a river rock wall, in an alcove that was nearly a cave, thanks to its other wall being formed by a waterfall. She glared at the thundering water as if she longed to drown herself in it. Her high, classic cheeks were already wet. But he knew, certain as he breathed, the drops weren't from the waterfall.

That look. Her tears. They almost caused him to turn and leave her be. They cracked him open. Decimated his logic. Shattered his professional composure. If he stayed for a second longer, he knew what he'd be tempted to do. To say.

She looked up and saw him.

He took a tentative step.

She jerked as if he'd thrown an electric charge across the grotto. Her lips, moist with her tears and berry bright from her bites, parted on a gasp. She drew breath for words. Mark cut her off.

"He's an ass."

He closed on her by two more steps. She stumbled back and slammed into the wall. "Oh, God!" Mortification stabbed the words. She palmed her cheeks.

As her hands came down, Mark grabbed them. And wondered what the hell he was doing. He didn't care about the answer. He only knew he longed to wipe out that pain in her eyes. No, it was more than pain. It was loneliness. He recognized it too damn well. Easy enough, when it was the same desperate glint he confronted in the mirror every morning.

"He's an *ass*." He let her see his locked teeth now. "Don't you see that?"

"Of course I see it! He pulls crap like this all the time at home. Earth-shattering surprise, huh?"

He let her look everywhere but at him. He softened his grip, elated when she didn't pull away. "But that's the first time he's ever pulled that particular wad of crap."

Her grimace confirmed that. He nodded, barely battling the urge to find Johnson, tell him to forget the maturity lesson, and just go the fuck home. Baghdad wasn't a place for sixteen-year-olds, even if they walked around in bodies twice that age.

While he got distracted with that fantasy, Rose finally took notice of how they stood. He nearly had her locked against the wall. Their hands, still joined, were the only thing blocking their chests from touching. "Shit!" she cried. "Look... Senator...I apologize—"

"What the hell for?"

She shook her head. "It's clear I can't handle this. Apparently I can't handle much of anything. I'm a mess. I'll save the company some money and go home now."

"The fuck you will."

She actually glared at him for three seconds. She seemed stunned he'd use that word, that tone, or both—making her response, calm as morning mist, even more a shock.

"The fuck I won't."

She dropped her head and tried to pull free from him. She had a snowball's chance of succeeding. "Rose," he reprimanded. "*Rosalind.* Listen to me. Nobody deserves to be on this project more than you. Nobody's got their head in a better space than you. Do you hear me on this? Rose?"

The top of her head, while a captivating crown of shiny russet, was unreadable.

The trembles of her shoulders, turning to the shudders

brought on by sobbing, were crystal clear.

"Rose." He let out a weighted sigh. Then pulled her against him. "Oh, little pet, what is it?"

It was all he could not to give in to a tremor himself. Holy Christ, what was he doing? This protectiveness, this aching need to grip her and hold her... He hadn't felt like this for a living person since he and Heather had whispered their final goodbyes. After that day, he thought he'd never feel this way again. No, goddamn it; he'd vowed it. Best to just swear off the pain forever than risk ever going through that hell again. But here, it felt so perfect. So right. The only choice that made sense, even if it did make all this feel like jumping from a plane at thirty thousand feet without an oxygen mask.

With a deep inhalation, he spread his arms. Since their hands were still locked, Rose's followed along beneath. The action succeeded at making her his prisoner against the wall. She gasped. The sound hit him like a rocket, compelling him to lower his cheek. He scraped up Rose's tears with his beard while shifting his mouth, so all he had to do was whisper for her to hear.

"Let it go, pet. You've been holding it in for so long, haven't you?"

She trembled, still resisting. He understood. He waited. The significance of what he asked... It delved far beyond just the words he'd just spoken. He wanted her trust. To help shoulder a burden she'd carried so long, it likely felt like part of her. He practically felt her torment too. Surrender her burden to him and face the emptiness it left behind, or turn and run again...back to the safety of her life?

The safety.

And the loneliness.

Damn it, he wasn't going to make her choice easy. Or, if he was being honest, his. He'd been safe for so long now, opting for the easiest way to think and the most comfortable thing to do, which was usually too damn much. His relationship with Dasha had nearly been the sacrifice for it. He'd only redeemed himself with her by tossing "safe" overboard.

Maybe that would work here too. Maybe that was why fate had brought him here to begin with. Maybe he was here to show Rose the truth about running. It wasn't always the answer—and safety wasn't always the key.

And maybe in showing her, he'd push away the loneliness for himself too. Christ, if only for a few minutes...

He shifted his hold, positioning his hands to circle her wrists. Squeezed in a fraction tighter. "Let it go." He lowered his mouth to her nape, unable to resist the elegant curve of skin. "I'm here, honey. Let it go."

Rose whimpered. Her wrists twisted in his hold. But when he eased his grip, concerned he'd hurt her from the rush of fresh Dom in his system, she still made the sound. Her lips were taut and her gaze shimmered, telling him one thing as clear as the sunshine of which she smelled. He hadn't pushed her physically at all. He'd rammed home a thousand emotional buttons—and now they all went off at once, overwhelming her.

Triumph surged. Yes. This was what she needed. Mental gears locked into place as he sensed it, knew it, savored it. He'd only just met her, but he *knew* her. He also knew he was meant to be here, to give her what she craved but wouldn't give to herself. Her worth to the world. Her beauty, within and without. Her desirability, an organic thing from her mind and her spirit, just as much as her incredible curves and her porcelain skin.

"That's it." He spread his legs, bracketing her body with his, rejoicing as she softened beneath him. "Don't fight it anymore. You don't have to. I'll be here to catch you, I promise."

"I...I can't..." It dissolved into a sobbing hiccup. "This...this isn't—"

"Anything or anyone but you and me." He murmured his next words against the furrows in her forehead. "I'll stop any time you want. Just say the word. But I don't think you want to stop, Rose."

She let out a sigh. Her breath flowed against his chest, spreading warmth through his center. Or was the heat already coming from within, stoked by her stunning, instinctive submission? He held his breath, fighting primal reflexes screaming for release from their long dormancy. Maybe this wasn't real. Maybe it was a dream. And if it was happening, maybe he'd overstepped and just exposed himself to drastic scandal. Or worse yet, had messed Rose up when all he wanted to do was help her, heal her. His gut clenched already at that—

Until the next moment, when she lifted her thick, velvet gaze again. "No. I don't want to stop. Please."

The words unhinged him. He tore the rest of her appeal from her lips with the crush of his. A sound, high and soft and needing, vibrated up her throat and into his. It urged him deeper, and he went there, with no backward thoughts or remorse, taking her sweet, brave surrender and sparking it into something greater when met by his command. Something higher and hotter...

She seemed to melt from one moan to the next, going fluid as a chocolate bar in the sun as he meshed their fingers and twined their tongues. He surged closer, fitting their bodies together. As he'd hoped, the ridge of his cock fit perfectly against the apex of her thighs. She was soft and pliant...perfect and sublime. Did she sense the same thing? God, he hoped so. Prayed she knew this was about much more than the lust slamming their bloodstreams...that it went beyond even their awakening as people. It sliced to the needs of their spirits, calling to each other in a dance as deep as time. Flint and kindling. Thunder and lightning. Water and wind. Elements designed for give and take...for domination and submission.

Which meant, when she suddenly pulled away, it felt like ramming a glacier.

He let her free, of course. The second her muscles stiffened, he backed off on the grip. Within seconds she stumbled all the way across the grotto. Her shoulders rose and fell with her breaths. Her face contorted on a look of confusion and conflict.

"I'm sorry, Rose. I didn't mean to—"

"Stop! Don't!"

Deeper horror crossed her face, as if she'd transgressed some strange law merely with her outburst. She dropped her head, looking chagrined and so goddamned, adorably submissive. "I...I mean— It was just as much my fault, all right?"

"What?" He felt his stare turning to a glare. "Rose, for Chrissake—"

"You need to get back." She held out her hands as if to stop him, though he hadn't moved. "I'll go back to the meeting room later, to get my things."

"I don't have to get back to anything, and neither do you. I canceled the rest of the day."

She blinked. "Oh." Her brow creased when he chuckled. "What?"

Mark shook his head and cocked half a grin. "You really thought I'd treat those morons with a shred of civility after what they did to you?"

"They're not...morons. Not really. A little immature, maybe." She fidgeted as he switched back to a glower. "Okay, a lot immature."

"Which is going to get their ignorant asses killed when they hit Baghdad." He dragged a hand across his head. "Which I so wish I was kidding about."

"Then they're lucky to have you, right?"

There was genuine care in her voice. It dunked him in amazement. Despite everything Johnson and his posse had put her through, she still cared about their well-being on this project. He didn't know whether to kiss her for that or turn her over his knee and redden her delectable ass. He strongly favored the latter, though he opted for impaling her with a hard stare and stating, "You want to help them? Then get your backside into training again tomorrow, Miss Fabian, and lead by example."

Spurred by the conviction, he closed the distance between them again and reclaimed her hands in his. "I'll be there every minute, Rose. I won't let you fall under their ax again. I promise."

After a long silence, she finally answered. "I know."

"And the sky is fucking chartreuse." He slipped a hand up to her nape. "You want to try again at convincing me you mean that, pet? Or perhaps you'd like to tell me what you're really afraid of."

He didn't know what possessed him to issue the order. He knew what she'd give as a response. Sure enough, that truth seared him from the depths of the gaze she lifted again

SIGH

to him, intense as a nuclear core and equally merciless. She didn't speak it aloud. She didn't have to. But he forced himself to do the deed, tightening his grip on her nape as he did. This incident was clearly going to be the first and only time they were together like this, but he'd be damned if he didn't follow through on his obligation as the Dominant here, handling the hard stuff as well as the simple.

"Rose. *Rose.* Why are you afraid of me?"

She blinked again—once more slamming invisible shutters over her gaze.

"I'll see you in class tomorrow, Senator."

He tried, and failed miserably, not to watch the beautiful curve of her backside as she turned—leaving him with the water crashing in his ears and his senses flooding his logic.

CHAPTER FOUR

"You're not afraid of him."

Rose drilled the thought aloud at herself as she tied her running shoes with hard tugs.

"You're not afraid of him."

The words came with more conviction. She was *not* afraid of Mark Moore. When she thought of him, even during those minutes when he'd pinned her against the wall in the waterfall grotto, it wasn't fear that filled her.

God help her.

Not fear.

The feelings had soared beyond that. Flown to a realm filled with just one word.

More.

She'd wanted more of his grip on her wrists. More of his tongue in her mouth. More of his body against hers, his voice in her ear, his strength commanding her. More of the snap in her mind as he'd overwhelmed her body. The freedom that came like she'd been living her life in a cage before now and he was a trainer with a whip, ordering her to leap out and fly for him.

Yes, for *him.* Because every height she gained was the key to his pleasure too. She'd felt it in every flexed muscle of his body, every coiled inch of his control, every rough note in his voice. He'd become an animal too. Primal. Passionate. Everything she'd been fantasizing about from him and more…

There it was again.

More.

"You're not—"

She stopped as she opened the door to her room. The setting sun blazed into her eyes as the truth burned across her mind.

She forced herself to say it aloud.

"You're afraid of what *you* are when you're with him."

She started her run, skipping a warm-up in favor of a pace designed to ditch the demons in her head. But the monsters wouldn't shake off. Her confession gave them the perfect fissures to dig in at her psyche.

You're afraid of what you *are when you're with him.* And what was that?

All the things she couldn't allow herself to be. Soft. Moist. Pure feeling. Pure need.

Oh God...especially need.

She bumped up her pace. If she couldn't fry the thoughts away by force of will, she'd drown them in sweat and pain. Good plan—until a cramp clawed her calf. Luckily, she was approaching the fitness center. She'd stop in there and grab several swigs of water while stretching out the cramp.

The resort's gym was spacious, well stocked, and empty. No surprise. It was the middle of happy hour, and everyone was likely in the cantina downing twofers of the resort's fruity, watered-down special of the day.

She headed for the cooler in the corner, well stocked with chilled water bottles. As she got one out and then dipped into a low stretch, somebody emerged from one of the locker areas on the opposite side of the room. At the same second, her calf decided misery was company, and her hamstring seized too. She collapsed to the seat of a weight machine, grimacing hard.

"Mother of a shitfaced bastard!"

With her eyes closed, she only felt, rather than saw, the approach of the room's other occupant. But the agony in her leg took precedence over putting on a friendly face for them. They'd get the idea fast enough. Woman writhing here, buddy. Just a friendly attack of cramps. Nothing to see. Move along, move along.

"I must admit, you redefine the world of swear words, honey."

His voice, rough and a little humored, was a pull cord on her gaze. She only hoped she controlled her reaction to appear like mild surprise instead of the awareness flooding her body. She looked up first, for that was where his statement had come from. There was only empty air. A touch behind her knee pulled her sights back down. There was Senator Mark Moore, down on one knee, assessing her with a focus that, at first stare, seemed purely medical. There was just one major exception. No doctor ever cranked her bloodstream from simmer to boil with a single touch.

No. She couldn't let herself turn into *that* woman again. The one who terrified her. The unthinking, incoherent, utterly stupid one.

Time to activate the prevention plan. Black humor was a good first step. "Yeah. That's me. Miss Memorable. I'm a walking USB stick."

"All right." His eyes warmed, not that she noticed. "If you say so." He ran his hand farther up, pressing into the bottom of her thigh, increasing his pressure though she let out a hiss of pain. "It's got you from toe to torso, doesn't it? Probably hurts a bit."

"You think?"

"Don't get testy. I'm trying to help."

"By turning your fingers into binder clips? Owww!" She tried to yank away as his grip found the meat of her cramp. But he locked his other hand to her ankle, securing her leg in place. "Please...stop...trying to help!"

The man only focused deeper on her muscle. If she weren't in such pain, Rose would've enjoyed this chance to see him at a closer angle. His face, slightly tanned, had enticing smile and laugh lines at his temples and cheeks. His skin gleamed a little from his workout, as did the gym-ad muscles of his arms and chest, which she had no choice but to notice thanks to his fitted gray tank top. He was power and grace combined, a man sure of where his body fit in the world, of where *he* fit in the world. She hoped a little of it would seep into her by osmosis, as he continued the relentless pressure on her leg. To feel like she fit—anywhere—seemed the magic unicorn of her life. Unattainable.

"Do you get these cramps a lot?"

His tone remained as clinical as his scrutiny, so the answering blip in her heart rate made no sense at all. "Only when I don't warm up before a run."

"And you didn't warm up this time? Why?"

"I—" *Needed to get away from thinking about you.* "I was impatient to get started."

A smirk curved his lips.

"What?"

He paused his ministrations—which weren't actually necessary anymore. The cramp had vanished—though surely he knew that too, having felt her muscles loosen. So why didn't he move his hands?

"You. Impatient," he replied to her charge. "Makes sense now that I know you a little better, but it's a far cry from three days ago."

"Oh?" She tried pulling away. He held on tighter. "I'm funny now, huh?"

"In a number of enticing ways, yes."

The creases at his temples deepened, officially taking his face from distracting to captivating. "When I first saw you come into the classroom on Monday, I thought of a Victorian cameo. A lady of the aristocracy. You moved like you had books on your head and not a care in the world."

He spoke the words as caresses, but they wreaked the opposite effect on her composure. Guilt punched in. Without even trying, she'd let someone down again. That someone was him—which somehow seemed the worst part of it.

"Well, sorry for the disappointment."

"I didn't say I was disappointed."

"Good." She had no idea why she still felt so defensive. And nervous. "Impatience isn't a sin."

"You're right. It's not. It can even be helpful, given the situation." His features tightened. His gaze, burning with all the colors of the hazel spectrum, narrowed. "But one of those situations isn't neglecting your well-being, Rose. You should have warmed up before running. You got off easy; this is only a couple of cramps. What if you'd seriously injured yourself? What if—"

"All right, all right." She held up her hands. "Got it, Coach."

The second the nickname popped out of her, his expression went from irked to thunderous. He dropped his hands and stood. "I'm glad you do, brat."

The word stung. But his physical retreat...was agony. She only had herself to blame, but flipping the anger back at him was the only choice for her sanity. "Look, I appreciate your... concern. But I've been taking care of myself for a long time, and—"

"Maybe that's exactly your problem."

She glared. "My care isn't your concern, sir."

He stared back—with a new blaze in his eyes making no sense at all. Just as nerve-racking was how he shifted again as she rose, moving with the intent of a lion tracking a zebra. "Maybe your care does need to be my concern."

"And maybe I just need to get out of here."

It was her parting shot. She meant it. This coincidence— seeing him again, sweaty and prowling and volatile—it was never supposed to happen, to mix with *her* like this, when she was punchy and in pain. Not the pain of her leg either. It was the torment of her psyche, taunting her every minute, now that he'd come along, pinned her to a wall, and all but ordered her to hand her will over to him. And damn him, making her believe, just for a few minutes, he could actually do something with her mess. Even heal it.

Fool.

The man had made his name in the senate for his ambition, tenacity, and big plans, but her rat's nest of self-esteem was beyond even his magical reach.

It really was time to go.

She pivoted and headed for the door.

"Damn it, Rose."

His bellow echoed through the room—and stopped her. Wheeling back around, she narrowed a stunned gaze. "*Why* are you yelling?"

"And why the hell are you so afraid of me?"

"Well, why do *you* keep pushing *me*?"

"*Because*, damn it." He'd done the stealthy-lion thing again. He was just a foot away, arms curled at forty-five-degree angles, veins standing out on his huge muscles. Again that damn invisible-tether look. "Because I see what you don't." His lips barely moved with the words. His gaze urgently raked her face. "Because you're worth so much more than you see, than you allow yourself to be given, than what you believe—"

"Don't." It spilled from her, as hot and humiliating as her tears. "Don't you dare make me go there. I've been there already, Senator, remember? And before Owen Dearborn, I'd been there a few thousand other times too." A bitter laugh broke free. "Mother always phrased it best. 'It's best you stop reaching for the fruit on the high branches, Rosalind. Your arms aren't long enough.' Well, I now know what fruit is appropriate for me. And it's fine. I'm fine."

"And you're wrong."

Just three words. But he stamped them with the same ferocious force overcoming his whole body as he grabbed her by the elbows. "You're wrong, Rose. *She's* wrong."

He gripped her much harder than he had that afternoon. The pressure, along with the heat flowing off him like sun flares, should've sent alarms through her. A normal woman would've evaluated the situation and been at least a little scared.

But Rose was wet. Aching. Her lips parted as her body hit the Override button on her brain. Every inch of her tingled in greeting to his nearness. She throbbed in need of his power. Her sex pulsed. Her heart fluttered. Her very skin came alive with craving...

More.

"What are you going to do?" Her dry rasp swirled through the inches of air between them. "Pin me to a wall again? Hold me down until I'm brainwashed to your will?"

Please hold me down again...

He didn't do that.

Actually, he...smiled.

Slowly. Knowingly. Confidently.

In the three seconds he took to curl it, everything changed between them. The air shifted, as if the moon pulled rank and called the tide back out to sea, where it could break free without the limits of the shore.

Ridiculous.

Beyond ridiculous.

Did you really just compare the man to the sun and *the moon?*

Rose, Rose, Rose.

He's forbidden fruit, girl. Don't play this high. You're going to fall and get hurt!

"No," he finally said, dipping the molten heat of his stare along the length of her body. "We've done the wall already, pet. And it clearly didn't make a difference in your mindset."

He tugged her closer. Her breath caught. Her head spun. "I...I hadn't thought that was the...intention."

The last syllable was nothing but a sigh, a breath mingling with his, as he dipped his head and lips near. "So you've been thinking about it?"

"Thinking about wh-what?"

"The wall. This afternoon. Being trapped. Being controlled. By me."

"Of course not!" She turned her face away. He followed without hesitation or mercy, pressing his mouth against her cheek, scuffing her skin with his beard, scratching deeper into her mind, whether she wanted it or not.

"I think you're lying. I think you've been thinking about it all afternoon. Just like I have."

His confession messed her thoughts more. "What are you

doing to me? Why do you *want* to do this to me? We can't... I can't..." She choked to a stop as his mouth traced closer, thickening the mental fog. She couldn't go back to that place again. She wouldn't. "Please...Senator... Mark..." She huffed. What the hell did she even call him anymore?

"Sir will do, Rose. I love the word when it comes off your lips. Especially when they're this flushed and beautiful."

He raised a hand and ran a slow thumb along her mouth. Confusion stormed her mind, body, senses. "F-For one thing, m-my lips aren't beautiful...and...and—"

"And that's a perfect place to start."

He didn't give her a second to breathe, let alone argue. Not when he took her mouth in one bold sweep of passion. He opened her at once, filling her with his tongue and even his teeth, shredding all the logic she had left. Rose tried to break free, but he seemed to expect that too. He buried his hand in her hair, securing her in place as he plunged, sucked, crushed, commanded—until, when he finally did break away, she actually gasped from the loss.

But he stole that too. Her gasp climbed into a shocked cry as he hoisted her into his arms and then strode deeper into the gym with her.

"What the hell?"

"I think you mean, what the hell, *Sir*?" He plunked her down on a padded sit-up bench.

"Wh-What?"

She might as well have spouted Swahili for all the care he gave the retort. She was too stunned to move, watching him stalk to a rack with a dozen jump ropes and then wrench half the inventory off their pegs. "Why are you... What's..."

"Are you *now* ready to tell me you how beautiful your mouth is?"

He stood in front of her again. His legs were braced, and a pair of the jump ropes were now stretched between his hands. Despite his ominous stance, she glowered. "No! What do you think—"

"Suit yourself."

His serene intonation gave her no clue about his intention. Before she blinked again, he twisted a rope around one of her wrists, crisscrossed it, and then captured the other arm too. He pulled that truss tight with one hand and then looped the second rope through the small gap between her wrists. Once he was able to hold her tight with one hand, he grabbed her waist with the other. His hold relayed pure strength, solid control, and no patience for a struggle. Still, Rose couldn't believe she complied without a word as he turned her over and laid her flat on the bench. Her face was down, and her arms were stretched over her head. Mark looped the rope around the bench peg, securing her into that position.

"This is crazy. What do you think—"

"The subject isn't me right now. It's you."

She pivoted her head to glare at him but was stopped short by his face, now tilted and just a few inches away again. And the look on it...was a transformation. A spell of golden magic. His mouth twitched with sexy-as-hell adoration. His eyes were twin hearths of warmth and wonderment. The bastard made it damn hard to figure out what she felt right now. Pure fury or pure fascination?

"What in all of *hell* are you doing?"

He actually looked like he fought back a chuckle. "Hmm. Not as interesting as your previous outbursts, but still enchanting. Especially because you'll be issuing no more statements like it for a while." She drew breath to tell him where he could go with that pomposity, but he jammed two fingers against her lips. "I said no more, Rose. Let me explain myself. I'm not going to hurt you. You know that as well; I don't see a speck of real mortal fear in your face. What I'm asking right now is that you trust me. That you acknowledge I've been a few steps in life farther than you, that I see an important lesson you can learn here, but that restraining you may be the only way you'll pay attention and absorb this knowledge."

His features intensified as he stroked a hand down her back. "If you don't agree, now or at any time, then you say the word. I'll let you up, and things return to normal between us. But that word isn't 'no.' Or 'stop.' You'll have to work harder, think harder, than that. Your word is 'worth.' Since you find it impossible to think of the term, let alone apply it to yourself, then it's a perfect word upon which you can focus." He finally released his fingers from her lips as he slipped his other hand beneath her shirt. His touch was a series of light, magical strokes against her skin. "Is all this clear? Do you understand?"

Her breath only cooperated in shallow spurts. He was right. He wouldn't physically hurt her. His touch on her back alone, steady but gentle, proved it. The only trouble was, she wanted him to press harder. She yearned for the raw, rough command he'd exerted this afternoon, trapping her against the wall. God, didn't that make her some kind of sicko? She knew what they called it. Submissiveness. The kink thing. *Weird.* She wasn't any of those things...was she? She was raised to be the perfect North Shore wife. She wasn't supposed to know about things like that, let alone like them.

But maybe Owen had seen just that. Had realized the wicked mistake fate made in her. Maybe he'd just known, after that night when they'd finally been alone in the suite at the Fairmont, and she'd dared to let him see a little of her true desires...

Maybe he'd gotten it right way before everyone else.

She was wired wrong. Plain and simple.

"Rose." He broke into her thoughts with the ramrod of a syllable. "Thoughts *here*. Right now. I won't ask so politely next time."

"Yes, Sir."

Though she grumbled it, he actually smiled. Best of all, he turned his caress on her back into a stronger, rougher possession. "That just flows from you, doesn't it?" He shook his head, as if bewildered. "Such a natural, and you don't even know it. Oh, Rose. Sweet Rose."

His gaze followed the path of his hand down to her lower back, sliding along the curve above her buttocks. He stopped for half a second before tucking his fingers beneath the band of her running shorts.

They both held their breaths. Rose almost held back her next words. Giving voice to them... It would likely take them across an unseen bridge, deeper down the sensual path he'd let her peek at this afternoon. She was terrified. And yet, it would've been easier to hold a burning match behind her lips.

"A natural...at what?"

When he gave her nothing but another enigmatic tilt of his lips, she frowned.

"Are you really not going to let me up unless I do what you say?"

His stare traveled down her body. His study was slower this time. Deliberate. "That's the plan."

She could hear herself breathing now. "Unless I say stop."

"Unless you say *worth*."

"Whatever. I can use it at any time, right?"

"I don't think you will."

He molded his hand around one of her butt cheeks. Rose gasped, jerking away by sheer instinct, shooting a what-the-hell gape again.

He didn't relent his hold by a centimeter.

She still didn't utter a word.

"You have a lovely ass too, Rose. It fits perfectly against my palm. And it's getting warmer. Everything down here is."

He was right about that too. Oh God, he was right. As he curled his fingers against her skin, kneading one buttock and then the other, deep shivers of pure heat spiraled into her upper thighs, down to her knees and her toes, and then back up again, centering in a pool of liquid magma right between her thighs. It was all she could do not to buck and squirm, simultaneously wanting to flee him and beg him for more.

She whipped her face away, digging her forehead into the bench pad. If her ass was that hot, everything from her neck up must be the shade of ripe turnips. "Oh God!"

He dug his fingers in a little harder, nipping the meat of her ass. "Not what I want to hear, pet." Though the words chastised, his tone was nearly a knight's courting croon. "Turn your face back to me so I can see you say the words. 'My mouth is beautiful.'"

She was so tempted to give him a snarl, the safe word, or both. But part of her, a growing part, wanted to simply lie there in silence, pushing his patience, wondering what he'd do if she did. The part refusing to be without his warm, knowing touch ever again.

"Fine!" She flipped her face back toward him. "My mouth is beautiful." She deliberately rushed it. "Pleased with yourself?"

Ridiculous question. The man beamed. "Of course. But I'm more than happy to share my pleasure, honey."

He'd barely drawled it all before dipping his fingers deeper between her legs. The contact with her sex only lasted a second but hit her like the tap of a wizard's wand. Every nerve in her clit pulsed. Energy zapped through her body. A cry escaped before she could help it.

"Easy, sweet Rose. We're not done yet."

The hell we aren't.

"I—this—I can't—"

"Of course you can. And you will." He coaxed her head back down by pulling the elastic band free from her ponytail and then spidering his hand against her head. "Next you're going to tell me, 'My *body* is beautiful.'"

"This—this is crazy! What if somebody comes in here and—"

"That's my concern, not yours." He worked more magic into her scalp and ass with his kneading, exploring hands. "Now don't you have something you'd like to tell me?"

She huffed. Again he pinched her ass in reprimand, once on each cheek. The brief pain acted like a switch in her brain. Her attention funneled on him—on what he'd requested of her. No, on what he'd ordered of her. And how much she yearned now to obey. To once more bring that incredible, radiant smile to his face...

"I...my body...is beautiful."

She didn't rush it this time.

Because it didn't feel stupid this time.

It felt...

Amazing.

Like it could be the truth.

"Rose." His reply was low and husky. "Your body *is* beautiful."

Just like that, he pulled her across another unseen bridge—and then burned that passage down behind them. Rose saw it in the transition in his face, his jaw jutting and nostrils flaring. She felt it in her most intimate core, deep inside, sending tiny streams of need down into her pussy. She shook from the inside out. Moaned aloud from its force.

He made things worse—and better—when he withdrew the hand in her hair and dipped it beneath her shorts as well.

"Lovely." He cupped an ass cheek in each hand. For the first time, Rose resisted her bonds. His touch was torment and enchantment, sending a thousand tingles through her body. Her skin didn't feel like enough coverage for her feelings anymore. She bucked and writhed, sure she was going to fall apart.

"Sshhh. Breathe. *Breathe.*"

How was it that his voice saved her from the very torture he inflicted?

"Focus on me, Rose. Listen to my voice. Focus on what I want you to say next."

Huh?

He wanted her to say more, to actually form words, when he rolled his thumbs deeper into the crevice between her legs and started spreading her there?

"Oh," she whispered. "Ohhhh…" No. She couldn't do anything beyond that. Impossible. Forget it.

"'My desire is beautiful.'" He directed it just as he opened her wider, pulling open the flesh of her sex so he could lightly stroke her there. "That's what you'll say next, pet."

"M-My—"

He found the button at her core. Flicked the sensitive strip of flesh.

Her cry became a scream.

"Beautiful. Truly beautiful, Rose. Do you want more?"

"God, yes. Please. Yes!"

"Then give me the words. Say it. 'My desire is beautiful.'"

Damn him.

Bless him.

She licked her lips and tore through her senses for a couple of rational thoughts to string together. "My...my desire... is beautiful."

"Oh yes, honey. It is."

He slid a second finger against her pulsing nub. This time he didn't release the pressure. Rose's head jackknifed back. Her sex turned to lighter fuel, and his fingers were matches. Everything was white heat and pure need. She pitched herself back as far as she could but didn't get very far, tethered in place by his deftly tied knots. Another cry ripped past her locked teeth.

"More, honey?" His own voice was tight and rough. He pivoted to kneel behind her, pulling her shorts down as he went, giving him uninhibited access to her dripping sex. "You need me to go faster? You want me to touch you harder? Do you need my fingers here, on your wet clit...your aching pussy?"

He unraveled the rest of her with the words. Her inhibition spun free from the spindle of her mind, dissolving into rasps of arousal and joy. "Yes. Yes. Yes please, Sir."

She heard his hiss, which seemed a mixture of joy and shock in itself, before his touch took on an urgent life of its own. "Very, very good, Rose. Now, just one more, sweetheart. Let me hear you say it. 'My surrender is beautiful.'"

Was he serious? "I...I— Ohhhh...mmmm..." She was ready. *So* ready. Her walls clenched all the way to her womb. She needed release...freedom from this ache...

"Give it to me, pet. *Now.* Say it to me and mean it— and when you're done, you're going to come hard. Do you understand, Rose?"

CHAPTER FIVE

His heart beat in time to Rose's frantic nods. Despite that, every sound from his own body was mute to him. With one slice of his brain still heeding the door, he focused the rest on her. Every nuance of her breath. The flush of her skin. The tension of her wrists against the rope, even the rhythm of how she tossed her hair on her back. He gauged everything about her...

Everything.

She intoxicated him.

She obliterated him.

She'd awakened him.

His Dom was back. Even if just for this exquisite, extraordinary moment...he was Master once more. At one with his sweet sub. Honored by her incredible gift. Determined to give it back to her with pleasure she'd never fathomed.

Slowly, with unalterable authority, he directed her again. "Say. It. You can do it, Rose." He stroked the pouting lips of her perfect cunt, knowing the action teased her clit in all the right ways. "Say it for me, pet."

She felt like heaven. Her skin, soft and moist beneath his thumbs, vibrated. With every twitch, his cock kicked harder at his sweats. But as much as he craved release, this wasn't about his body. It was about the beast in his brain, the creature who'd lain dormant for far too long, rejoicing in its fiery rebirth.

"My...surrender...is beautiful."

"Yessss."

He blended his hiss to her rasp as he plunged a thumb into her tight tunnel. He needed to feel her from the inside out as he proved her words perfectly true. "You remember what I want you to do now, Rose?" He watched her try to nod as the rest of her body took over, hips gyrating, her ass a mesmerizing landscape. He curled his other hand against her sex. The hard, hot ridge of her clit was his greeting committee. As he teased that quivering bundle of nerves, she keened and shivered.

"That's it," he coaxed. "You're so ready, aren't you?"

"Yes," she cried. "Yes. Please!"

"Then come for me. Don't hold back. Come, Rose. Now!"

Her scream, full and strident, filled the air. Her scent, tangy and heady, flooded his senses.

Her tears ripped at his heart.

Gritting back words that would only sound empty, he simply continued stroking her. Watched as she rode the release, along with the emotions it freed—until he couldn't any longer. Not as she kept sobbing.

He leaned over, quickly releasing her from the rope and then tugging her shorts up before pulling her into his lap. She snuffled and fumbled, as if not knowing what to do. He guided her arms around his neck, compelling her to lean on him as her heartbeat calmed. Holding her close was an invitation to a new paradise. She was so beautifully made, with generous curves to her hips and ass. Her breasts, even tucked beneath a sports bra, pillowed against his chest with delectable softness.

"What a woman you are." He rasped it against her neck. "Thank you, Rose, Thank you."

She pulled back a little. Huffed and wiped at her eyes. "Uhhh, isn't that my line?" She scooted back even farther, glancing down. The evidence of her effect on him still stood stiff in his crotch. Her direct gaze didn't help matters. He cleared his throat, fighting the urge to adjust his balls to a more comfortable tension. She cleared her own. "And shouldn't I be showing you my thanks instead of telling you?"

Before he could stop her, she dropped to the floor between his knees and reached for his waistband—until Mark stopped her, seizing her hands. "Is that what you think I want?" At her startled blink, he tamped down a surge of fury. Of course she thought that. A wedding day that never was, coupled with the genetic chip for taking responsibility for the world, had churned out a woman who "proved" her worth to a man with her mouth between his thighs.

He pulled harder, making her sit beside him. "No. Not right now. Come here."

Confusion bunched her brows. "You...don't want me to..."

"Oh, pet. Clearly there's nothing I'd want more. But right now, this isn't about me. This is about you, talking about what's happening in those rooms in your head—most particularly, the one where all the waterworks came from."

Her frown deepened. Those full berry lips gathered into a puzzled pout—*not* helping him forget how gorgeous she'd been on her knees, between his thighs.

"I don't have 'rooms' in my head."

"Oh yes you do." He swung a leg over so he straddled the bench. "Why the tears?" He ran a hand across her cheek. "I didn't hurt you, did I? Were the ropes too tight?"

"The ropes were fine." She grabbed his hand with a desperate urgency. "I... The ropes were..." She sucked in a harsh breath. "The ropes were wonderful."

Understanding set in. The dip of her head, along with the

way she sounded like she'd just confessed murder to a priest, made him nod. "Ah. And you're conflicted about that. A little overwhelmed?"

She tapped at his knuckle with a dainty fingernail. Though the polish was light pink, each nail had a little dark-pink jewel glued on it. Hmm. His Victorian cameo girl had a secret thing for bling. And, they were both quickly learning, for other alternative things. Trouble was, the lesson was turning her into a giant ball of nerves. That mass was likely infused with fear too.

"Look, I've got a couple of girlfriends into the bondage-and-submission thing. A few times, I even went to a club with one of them."

"And?"

"And what?"

"Did you enjoy it?"

"It was fine. But all I did was watch. And it was...fine." She stammered it out like the priest had locked her in the confessional for a boldfaced lie. Which looked to be pretty much the case. "But just not my..." She huffed. "Look, I'm not some closet kinkster, okay?"

"Pity," Mark replied. "Because I am."

That got her attention. Newly stabbed by her wondering stare, he leaned in until their noses were inches apart. "There's nothing wrong with it, Rose. It's a beautiful gift that you give, in following your need to surrender. A man is hardwired to take care of his woman, in all ways and forms. Some of us just like to be more in control of the process. *Much* more in control. And when a woman trusts enough in our control to submit fully, such as letting herself be restrained and guided to fulfillment... to a Dominant, that's like water from heaven." He closed the gap, taking her lips in a tender caress. "It's a drink I haven't had for a very long while." He moved the kiss up, gently bussing the end of her nose. "Thank you."

She sighed, brushing fingers along his beard, but then shook her head. "This feels so incredible. But it can't be right."

"Why?" He grabbed those fingers. "Are you seeing someone?"

A laugh shot from her. "No! God, no. There's no one." She sobered. "But surely you—"

"No one." He said it with deliberation, needing to wipe the disbelief from the back of her gaze. "Sweetheart, despite the antics of some of my coworkers in Washington, bed-hopping never has, and never will, hold much appeal." A deep chuckle emerged. "Believe me, it really *has* been a long time."

"You're kidding me."

He squeezed her nape. "Not about this." When she looked away, he clamped the hold tighter. "You still don't believe me?"

"No. I believe you. It's just that—"

"What?"

"Well, you're on the younger side for Washington, which has to make you prime meat on their invitation lists." Her cheeks turned the color of her name. "And you're hot as hell."

The annoyance turned into a laugh. "I'm glad you think so. You're pretty goddamn hot too." The delicious curves of her mouth called to him again. He molded their lips and tongues together, diving his hand into her hair when she started pulling away, holding her for his consummation. Too late. Though her mouth complied, the rest of her form resisted. When he slackened his hold, she lurched to her feet.

"No. Please." She pressed shaking hands to her cheeks. "We have to stop wanting this. We have to stop thinking it can happen!"

Mark shut his eyes. It was time to grab the room's elephant by its big, fucking, floppy ears. "Because despite the hotness factor, I'm still older."

She flung her hands out. "For one thing, yes. But—"

"I'm forty-five, Rose. And you're...what..."

"Thirty-one."

He gave her a gentle smile. "It's not unheard of. And we're not teenagers, sweetheart. Bogart and Bacall were twenty-five years apart. Harrison Ford and Calista Flockhart? Twenty-two years. Rhett Butler had a twenty-year jump on Scarlett O'Hara."

She scowled. "Fictional characters. No points on that one." And how did he just pull all of that out of his head?

"Two out of three, then. I've made my point."

"It's still— *You're* still—"

"What?" He rose calmly as he could while his patience still allowed. "I'm still what, damn it?"

"You're still you! Respected on Capitol Hill. Demanded by Fortune 500 players. The father of a major music star." She dodged his outstretched arms, gazing at him with half her bottom lip in her mouth and her heart glittering in her eyes—betraying to him, in one incredible second, how she'd been just as floored by what they'd shared so far. Yet in the next breath she whispered, "What's the expression they use? Out of my league. That's it. No. You're even beyond that. You're out of my universe. We can't let ourselves get deluded. Neither of us can afford it. Not now. Not ever."

Mark didn't stop at irritated now. He let fury stomp right in as he pulled her up next to him. "So that's it, then? The universe has gone through all this goddamn work to bring us together like this, giving us this gift, practically pounding us over the head with how perfect this is, and you're going to hide behind all these excuses?"

"Not excuses." She pushed at his chest. "Reasons. Good ones!" When her escape effort didn't work, she huffed. "Look; I believed in the gift once. I believed in it all. I bought the whole glass-slipper fantasy, thinking I'd found my prince—"

"I'm not pretending to be a goddamn prince."

"I know that."

"Rose." He bracketed her jaw between his thumb and forefinger, forcing her gaze up again. "I want to give you something better. Do you get that? Do you see it? You're already halfway there. Rose...pet..."

Her gaze pooled with new tears, giving him a glint of hope—before she tried to jerk away. "Stop calling me that! Why do you call me that?"

"Because it fits." He pulled her back next to him. "Because I want to take care of you, see after you. I want to meet every need you have and then some. And because you need it." He fitted her head to his neck, loving the way her lashes felt against his jugular. "You know it too, don't you? So why are you so afraid of it? Why are you denying who you are, who you clearly want to be? Why do you surrender so exquisitely for me but deny what makes you feel so good and blossom so beautifully?"

She turned her head so their eyes met again. He stared at her, nestled so perfectly against him, and endured a rush of amazement. He'd stuffed his life full of things seeming fulfilling...and all of it, with the exception of his time with Dasha, was like a washed-out painting compared to this. To simply holding a subbie after he'd taken her to heaven and back. No. It was holding *this* subbie. He longed to cradle her all night, to pull her tighter so he could kiss her deep...

She read his thoughts on that one. Rose sifted her fingers through his beard and then his hair, coaxing him lower, lower, until their lips met again. Fire and arousal roared through him anew, until the second he recognized the desperation behind the sweeps of her tongue and the pressure of her mouth. When they pulled apart, the depths of her gaze confirmed his suspicion. The kiss wasn't hello. It was goodbye.

"I have to deny it," she whispered. "I have to. Not every rose is meant to blossom, Senator. Some are just there to remind the world about the thorns."

She pushed to be free again. This time, Mark let her go—just like he let her leave the building without looking back. He found the strength to get through it by remembering a little axiom that had served him well through the years.

"You took the battle, Rose," he murmured. "But the war is far from over."

CHAPTER SIX

The next morning, Rose stopped in the hallway outside the meeting room to take a deep breath. Another. Her head already throbbed, due to one inescapable fact. Facing Ryan, Pete, Kai, and the others was less terrifying than having to face Mark Moore again.

She'd hijacked his beautiful words last night and driven them into the ground. To make matters worse, she'd turned and left him standing in the mental wreckage. Not that she didn't feel a hundred kinds of shit for it. Not that she hadn't stopped ten steps out the fitness center's door, longing to run back in and say she didn't mean it, that she'd never felt like this before, not even with Owen. And oh yeah, while she was at it, he was right; she was indeed a stubborn brat and needed to be put in her place. She needed to be tied back down and given over for his punishment...and pleasure.

God, how she wanted to bring the man pleasure.

Instead, she'd gone back to her room, caught *Titanic* on HBO, and then fallen into a chaotic sleep just before midnight. The irony of the whole thing hadn't escaped her. The Rose in the movie had been given a soul mate and then gone against everything she knew to have him. The ship hit the damn iceberg anyway.

But the woman had known a love for a lifetime.

She clenched her jaw, banished the thought, and forced her feet forward.

Her stare found him instantly. The experience was worse than she'd anticipated. In a rich charcoal suit and deep burgundy tie, with his hair and beard groomed to perfection, he looked beautiful enough to jump—yes, even here. His clothes, fitted to the millimeter, made him as perfect as a magazine ad— but his stance turned him into something more appropriate for a wild-game hunter. Every inch of him conveyed pure aggression, from his braced legs and stiff shoulders to the scowl tense enough to bite someone's hand off.

His expression intensified when he looked up and saw her.

She squared her chin, meeting his glare directly. He'd asked her to return, not the other way around. The intimidation-by-wounded-male bit wasn't going to work.

Bolstered by the conclusion, she marched her way down to the front of the room again. Without a hitch, took her front-row seat. She didn't look back up again until she'd stowed her purse and pulled out her course binder and pen—

And got assaulted by a stare more intense, permeating, and cocky than a grown man had a right to yield.

Which, coupled with the tie and suit, brought her right back to the whole craving to glue herself to him.

Until she noticed the smirk.

It was the smallest of expressions, a tiny sideways slant...

Maybe she'd just imagined it?

But then the bastard slid the look to the other side of his mouth.

The gig was up. His original glare really was a ploy—a stunt to draw her close like a magnet on metal shavings.

Why?

And why did she squirm when considering the answer to that?

Looking at him didn't help. His all-business mask was slammed back into place as he addressed the entire class.

"I hope all of you enjoyed the break yesterday and used it to accomplish the goals I set?"

Reactions ranged from awkward coughs to "Yes, Senator." It didn't escape Rose that Kai and Peter chose the latter response. Ryan chose stoic silence and a respectful nod to Mark, acknowledging he'd heard. Shockingly, he included her in the action too.

The *Twilight Zone* theme started in her head. Ryan Johnson, prick of the year, was giving *her* deference? What the hell had happened in here yesterday? A questioning stare back at Mark yielded nothing. His eyes had turned as hard as agates, and his mouth was set with grim satisfaction. His words from the grotto echoed in her head. *"You really thought I'd treat those morons with a shred of civility after what they did to you?"*

A strange warmth suffused her chest. Was this what those medieval maids felt when knights went out and broke lances on each other for them? And if so, did the damsel question the feeling as being completely ridiculous?

"Very good," Mark pronounced. She half expected him to pound his chest too, but the man's authority was subtler than that. He moved forward, once again to the desk right next to her. She braced herself for the sexy-as-hell, lazing-lion thigh pose from yesterday, but he went for something more commanding, hiking a foot up to the chair. "I believe we left off at discussing one's attitude in unknown lands. In short, leaving the office mentality behind, getting into the headspace of your guest status in another country. Can anyone share if they took away any keywords from our dialogue?"

Rose wasn't surprised when Ryan jumped on the chance

to speak. His tone conveyed the pure purpose of getting in a fresh piss on his territory. "Leadership."

"Okay," Mark answered. "Good. You thought about your answer, Mr. Johnson. That's an outstanding way to phrase it. Who else?"

Christine, one of Aria's buddies from the Austin office, raised her hand. "Compassion?"

"Excellent, Ms. Daye." He nodded at the back of the room. "And Ms. Vernon?"

"Humility." Veronica, from the New Orleans office, said it with conviction.

Mark gave back a hum of praise, bringing another heat front to Rose's chest. This time the sensation wasn't so pleasant. Okay, it was shitty—especially when she recognized it as a certain green monster of sentiment. It outright rankled when she let it drive her arm up.

"Ms. Fabian?" He cocked his head her way at once. "You'd like to share?"

She floundered. Everything about his posture was casual and relaxed. Everything about his stare was incisive and intense. But damn it, he wasn't going to crumble her so easily. She lifted her chin, deliberately defiant about the motion. "Brains, Senator. Plain and simple. People don't use them enough."

His brows lifted. "It's all about the head today, is it? What happened to yesterday's words of the heart?"

She took him up on the brow jump but added a shrug. "Heart still has its place, but not as your mission statement. When you're in new lands, where you don't know where you are or what lies ahead in the next hour, you can't just let everything go to the moment. You do that, and you're..."

He leaned toward her by just an inch. But even that tiny schism of space, filled with his presence, made her stammer into silence.

"And you're what, Ms. Fabian?"

Hell.

His stare sliced in, deeper and hotter. Confronting it was like standing naked in the summer sun—with all the resulting heat to the layers of her sex.

"You're...overwhelmed."

A smirk inched back across his lips. "Overwhelmed isn't bad, Ms. Fabian. Sometimes you can't, and you won't, control everything."

"So what, then? You surrender and get yourself killed?"

"Sometimes you surrender in order to survive. Sometimes surrender *is* your freedom."

Air was becoming a rare commodity to her lungs. He was so close. Too close. Too strong, hard, golden, and beautiful... and infuriatingly sure of himself.

Especially as she realized, with every instinct in her body, he wasn't talking about the mission anymore.

Damn him.

She fought his little trick with an irritated snap. "I respectfully disagree."

He reacted to that with leonine grace, returning to his feet in a couple of smooth steps. But his gaze, as hard as stone again, never left her. "Overwhelmed is inevitable." His voice drilled with the same unflinching intent. "It. Will. Happen. And the only thing you can do is be prepared, Ms. Fabian...to accept it."

She parted her lips a little, letting him see her locked teeth. "Accepting dangerous plans isn't what I do anymore, Senator."

"Then for the first time, I *am* worried about your fate on this project, Ms. Fabian."

Forget the emotional sunburn. He'd gone ahead and pulled out her spirit and fried it to a crisp.

As Rose blinked from the blow, Kai obliged the class by filling the air with a low whistle. "Oooh! Senator Moore throws down!"

"Shut up, Mr. Thomas."

"Yes, sir."

Mark gave her one last look, nearly dismissive in how icy it was, before looking out across the room once more. "All right, I want everyone at page fifty in your study manuals. We'll start in on daily rituals and project work habits until first break in a couple of hours."

CHAPTER SEVEN

If she checked her watch one more time, Mark was certain she'd bust the thing from overuse.

Under other circumstances, he would've chuckled at the way he'd clearly pushed some of her buttons. Correction: had nearly short-circuited the control panel she'd worn here this morning. And yes, he *would* have laughed at his handiwork—if that had been his intention. After secretly shadowing her back to her room last night to make sure she got there in one piece, he'd taken a walk on the beach, hoping to clear his head about the way things had gone in the fitness room. If he could dissect why he'd responded to her like that, going straight for discipline and domination, maybe he could purge the whole thing—and write it off as the aberration *she* kept insisting.

Instead, while replaying every second of the episode, all he'd done was enjoy it. Savor the rightness of it. The perfection of her submission. The beautiful notes of her climax and every gorgeous tear of her breakdown in his arms afterward. And yes, the glory of what she'd become and the triumph of what he'd discovered in himself again.

All of it. All over again.

Including the moment she'd bolted.

Damn it, he needed to talk to her again. He had to get back into her head, to figure out where her disconnect had occurred. He couldn't let her go on thinking there was something wrong with who she instinctively was created to be...all the joy she was meant to have...

Suddenly, the suit, the tie, and the room itself weren't the only things feeling too tight and hot. Even in her ire, maybe *especially* in it, she was a delicious mix of movement and attitude, arousing him with visceral force. He observed the feisty little stabs of her hands as she grabbed water and a tea bag from the catering table in their break patio and then bypassed the platter of doughnuts to press against a wall, brooding like she wanted her orange pekoe to turn into a murder dagger. Her nostrils flared. Her mouth was a twist of stewing-in-my-own-juices conflict.

She needed some time. His instinct bellowed it at him. A little time. A lot of patience.

He growled low. There was his damn rub. He had plenty of the latter and none of the first.

"None" didn't sit well in his vocabulary.

With renewed purpose, he strode across the patio as if needing to go check on something at the hotel's front desk, making sure his path took him past Rose. As he expected, she emitted a little snort. As he hoped, she tossed her tea and followed him.

"Senator!"

Her shout stopped him in front of the hotel's bar. The place was dark now, cleaned from last night's revelries, despite the air still hinting of spilled booze, sweaty bodies, and salty snacks. He paused, leaning on the empty hostess podium with a pretense of mild surprise.

"Miss Fabian. Hello. What's on your mind?"

On the other hand, no pretense in her. What thin veneer she had on her ire came off as she approached and then dug her nails into his arm with the force of a pissed-off sand crab.

She dragged him deeper into the murky room, glancing to

make sure they were alone. "I think you already know what's on my mind."

He tilted his head. "I'm many things, Ms. Fabian, but mind reader isn't one of them. And even if you're right and I do know, what makes you think I'd presume how you've processed your thoughts or would let you get away with not talking to me about it?" He savored the startled flare of her lashes and took advantage of tumbling her more off-center. With a deliberate step, he got close enough to make her head fall back. "Speak up. Let's hear it, pet."

"S-Stop calling me that."

He dipped his head a little more. "Have dinner with me tonight, and I'll consider it."

"That's extortion."

"That's negotiation." He couldn't help it. Her neck called to his fingers, so creamy and elegant. It felt like silk as he caressed from her ear to her collarbone. "And I'm very good at it."

Her breath hitched. She jerked back. Well, tried to. He was ready for the move and counteracted it by catching her nape and locking her in place. She countered with a harsh huff. "Okay, fine. You want me to talk? Here's me talking. What the hell were you trying to pull in there? Is that some kind of specialty test for the students you want to drive the craziest? Is that the reason for the special suit today?"

He willed everything south of his eyes into complete composure—forcing her to meet his gaze again. "I merely bridged off the answer *you* gave, Ms. Fabian. Extemporization is another handy skill for this project. I'm damn good at that, as well."

She folded her arms. "Extemporization is one thing.

Taking the conversation totally off subject and then toting it across the line you did is another."

"You're right." He curled his other arm around her, pressing his hand into the dip just above her delectable backside. "But I achieved my target goal, right?"

"Which would be...?"

"I'm standing here, holding you."

"Hmmph. So now am I supposed to congratulate you?"

Mark practically felt the furious thrum of her blood in every pulse through his veins. He looked at the copper tints in her eyes, betraying the awakening in her senses. He savored it all like getting to an oasis after four years of the desert. A rumble prowled up his throat. He pulled her closer. God, he loved the way she bent for him, innately soft and compliant beneath his strength.

"You're supposed to do whatever you want with me. Because, sooner or later, I'm going to do whatever I want with you."

He lowered his nose to her neck in time to feel her heavy swallow. Still she stammered, "Y-You're extemporizing into the realm of fantasy now, Senator."

"I'm very good at making fantasies come true, Ms. Fabian."

"Is there anything you're *not* good at?"

"Yes. Waiting." He joined his mouth to his cause, pressing a small kiss into her skin. "Have dinner with me tonight."

Her chest rose and fell. He felt her struggle to steady her pulse. "How about, 'have dinner with me tonight, *please*'?"

"How about, 'have dinner with me tonight, and I'll spare you an afternoon of further extemporization'?"

She laughed. At first. He savored how the vibration coursed along her neck, flowing into his beard and then his skin. Every second of it. Because all too soon...

She'd yank back like she did now.

"You're not kidding, are you?"

He closed back in on her. "Try me." There was nothing light in his words now. If she wouldn't give him credence in Romeo mode, he'd go straight to being Tybalt.

She was utterly still for a long moment. Only the depths of her eyes moved, exploring his face.

"Why?" she finally blurted. "What good is it going to do?"

"Because we need to talk. *Just* talk, Rose. You can't deny this. You can't ignore the way our bodies, our souls, shout to each other. We owe it to fate, to ourselves, to give it a fair conversation with no distractions. No double meanings. No noise. No waterfalls. No intrusions."

"No jump ropes?"

He brushed a strand of her mahogany hair from where it fell across her gaze. "You liked the jump ropes." Her hair was thick and warm against his fingers. He gathered more of it in his hold. "I think your word was *wonderful.*" Her throat tightened from his touch, a sight he watched in fascination. She was all over the place in her message now, and he savored the little victory.

"I also think red velvet ice cream is wonderful. That doesn't mean it's good for me."

With more calculated intent, he pulled back. She blinked, taken aback, further fulfilling his objective. "Suit yourself," he drawled. "I look forward to this afternoon's session, then."

She jerked her chin up, again a mesmerizing sight. "Maybe I'll just be sick this afternoon."

"And tomorrow morning too? And every day for the next six days?"

He could practically hear her teeth grinding. "Why are you being so—"

"What?" He pulled off his suit jacket, tossed it on the bar, and then did the same with his tie—all the while barely holding back a smile. Her torment, battling her honor of him as a teacher against her desire for him as a man, was a beguiling sight. "I'm not Senator Moore right now. I'm not your trainer or your superior. What *am* I, Rose?"

The curves of her face ignited with eager fire. "Obstinate," she declared. "You're being an obstinate, importunate, relentless—"

"Extemporizing." He finally gave in to the grin. "Don't forget that."

"Ass." she countered. "Yes. An ass. A man possessing one of the most brilliant and stimulating minds I've ever encountered, which can't seem to think its way past the fact that this"—she toggled a finger between both of them—"does not make sense! At all."

It was surprisingly easy to keep the grin going. "Thank you for your honesty. Now you're forbidden from saying that again until after dinner."

"Forbidden? Huh. Really? Says you and what? Your jump ropes again? Unless you conveniently packed your floggers for a just-in-case scenario..."

He let the smile fade. Took a step toward her. Just one. "You really want to push me on this, pet?"

"'Pet.'" She muttered it like referring to dog crap. "We're going to talk about *that* at dinner too."

"Perhaps we will."

His quiet tone coincided with Rose's heavy sigh. She'd just realized what she'd agreed to.

"Fine," she spat. "Where? What time?"

"I'll come for you. Eight o'clock." He couldn't help brushing her cheek one more time with his knuckles. "Thank you, sweet Rose."

"You're welcome, extemporizing ass."

CHAPTER EIGHT

The knock on her room door came at the stroke of eight. Rose expected he'd be on time but jumped anyway, swallowing back the nerves stampeding from her stomach to her throat.

"It's only dinner," she muttered. "And you're only going to talk. You're going to set him straight about why none of this makes sense, no matter how much his thunder sets off your lightning. You're going to tell him you're off-limits, and there's going to be no more tying up, pinning down, or senses getting stolen again."

Which was why she'd thought of nothing else all afternoon.

"Get. Over. it." She dropped her head in a sharp nod. "Don't beat yourself up. Just focus on what you need to say now."

Deep breath. Then another as she checked herself in the mirror. For the fifteenth time, she questioned her wisdom in choosing the outfit. It'd been a last-minute toss into her suitcase, as she was sure she'd never need something like the white wraparound skirt and matching one-shouldered blouse. The ensemble felt too revealing, but her only other choices were casual business sets, workout clothes, pool sarongs, and a couple of bathing suits. Since she had no idea where they were going for dinner, the Beyoncé-meets-Margaritaville look was the winner by default.

Skimpy clothes aside, she was resolved about throwing aside the obsessions of the afternoon and keeping her head snapped on straight tonight.

And her body? Officially cut out of the equation.

Stamping a professional smile on her face, she opened the door.

The smile dropped. An impeccable dark suit filled her doorway, but Mark Moore wasn't in it. The square-jawed guy with the military hair and the security radio in his hand gave her a deferential nod before speaking in a warm Texas drawl.

"Evenin', Ms. Fabian. I'm Brandt Howell, GRI security team. The senator got a bit hung up and asked me to come escort you to him."

She blinked. "Hung up? Is he okay?" And why did he have company security come get her instead of just calling and saying he'd be late? Dealing with this man was like navigating a very twisted road.

"Oh, yeah!" Brandt's grin took up half his face. "Totally fine. He just got to flapping lips with the big man, the way they always do, and lost track of the time. You ready?"

"Uh, yeah." She didn't have the guts to ask what he meant by "big man." Brandt seemed to think she already knew.

Her curiosity spiked with every step they took toward the part of the hotel where the larger suites and VIP villas were located. When they arrived at an arched, ornate doorway, she went ahead and let nervous back in to the party of her emotions.

The next second, nervous stepped aside for staggered. And to her horror, a case of utter speechlessness.

Brandt's "big man" was *the* big man. Dante Tieri, CEO of Global Restoration. She tried to imagine her eyes were a movie camera and she could just pull focus and change the sight, but the man's distinct, tall form was still parked on a couch opposite Mark, a tumbler of Scotch balanced between his hands, apparently enraptured by every word from Mark's lips. Mark took a sip from his own drink before cracking some quiet joke, making Mr. Tieri throw back his head with its famous thick and tumbling hair.

Rose scowled. Blinked. Gulped. Scowled harder. Was Mr. Arrogance really sitting there trading one-liners with Dante freaking Tieri?

"Ms. Fabian."

Mark's voice claimed the word, making it caress and command at once. Her blood went hot, and her nerves turned to icicles.

Somehow, she plastered the professional smile back on. "Good evening, Senator. I didn't mean to interrupt. I didn't realize you still were...uh..."

What? In a meeting? Flapping lips, as Brandt put it? Holding court, as *she* saw it? Sure explained the suit now. Damn, it had to be his thirteenth hour in the thing, and he still looked cool, impeccable, and chiseled as a Dolce & Gabbana ad too.

"You're not interrupting. Inferno Boy and I are just finishing up." His entire face warmed as he took her in, eyes crinkling and lips parting, before he pressed a hand to the small of her back and led her over to—

Inferno Boy?

There was an impression impossible to shake for a long time. Like forever.

"Mr. Tieri," she murmured. "Hello. I'm—"

"Rose Fabian." The head of her company had already gotten up and extended his hand. In the center of his face was the signature smile with which, according to the tabloids, he'd shattered supermodels' hearts across the globe. Now facing the full wattage of the look, Rose understood why. "I already know all about you," he said. "Mark's been singing your praises for the last hour."

"Dante." It was a reprimand. "My daughter does the singing, not me."

Tieri snorted. "Yeah. How could I forget?" He flashed *the grin* at her again. "Scratch the singing. You're still his star student." A wink followed, really more a kiss of the man's upper cheek to the corner of his eye. "And I'd like to thank you for it. Good work, Ms. Fabian. It's an honor to have you on the Baghdad team." After releasing her hand, he drawled, "Later, Marker Man. Thanks for the update. You're right. It was worth touching down from Venezuela. So let's go take that dive after you get back, yes?"

"As long as it's your turn to pick up the beer tab after."

"Right!"

Tieri drew out the vowel on that parting shot. He let himself out, taking Brandt with him.

Rose shifted from foot to foot. She was suddenly very much alone with Mark Moore. In a very large suite that felt very small.

He pulled off his jacket, his gaze never leaving her.

She followed every inch of the graceful action, feeling fifteen, infatuated, and ridiculous. *Again.*

All right, dinner would have to be skipped. It was time to just cut to the chase, get this whole skirmish over with, and then march her backside out the door. She couldn't stay, not when he already had her heart forgetting beats just because he'd shucked his jacket.

She needed some air. The slider to the patio and the garden was open. With careful steps, she made her way there. Cicadas sang in the trees, which waved in a breeze smelling of approaching rain. She glanced up to find Mark's stare still on her, silent and assessing. He barely moved—until she dashed her tongue over her lips. A small hiss erupted from his. She swallowed, tearing through her brain for something to fill the tightrope walk of a moment.

"Why did he call you Marker Man?" She said it with true curiosity, grateful she hadn't had to fall back on some inane comment about the weather. He shrugged, actually looking a little uncomfortable about the answer. Hmm. She'd knocked him off-kilter for once. The feat wasn't as satisfying as she thought it would be. His reply, however, earned an uptick of attention.

"Dante and I don't screw around with each other. Sometimes that makes us a couple of bulls in a china shop, especially when we're together. But it's also formed the base for a great friendship. One day we tossed some beers and indulged in some semidrunk emotional guy shit about it. He told me I was in his book in 'permanent marker.' We laughed like a pair of idiots about it, but it's stuck."

The story was pretty endearing. She told him so by tilting a smile at him as she stepped outside. Marker Man Moore and Inferno Boy Tieri, a bromance for all time."

"Repeat that to anyone, and I promise, no matter where you're at in the world, I'll come after you—and the floggers *will* be packed."

Her mind played out an image from his words. Him, bare-chested and rippling, swirling a pair of floggers through the air in beautiful symmetry. Her, spread and bound to one of those X-shaped crosses from the BDSM clubs, moaning and arching beneath the mixture of pleasure and pain.

She pulled in a sharp breath, hoping he hadn't heard, and

sat in one of the padded chairs next to the villa's private pool. Her panties, now seeping, decided to share their hydration with the apex of her thighs. Re-crossing only made matters worse.

New topic. Now. You're here to talk logic and reality, not succumb to chemistry. You're not one for the best odds where chemistry is concerned, Ro.

"So, you two go diving together?" Shockingly, she kept her voice even. "Where? In Lake Michigan? I've heard there's shipwrecks down there. That must be kind of fun. Do you live in Chicago now?"

He didn't make a move to sit with her. Instead, he slipped off his tie and then strolled to the slider that led to the bedroom and tossed the burgundy garment into the room. He didn't close the door when he was done. Still leaning against the jamb, he drawled, "You're quite the inquisitive thing tonight. Trying to skirt a subject, Ms. Fabian?"

"You didn't answer my question."

He looked out over the pool. "I live in Chicago now, yes. And yes to your second question as well. Sort of."

"Sort of?"

"Yes, Dante and I dive."

"In Lake Michigan?"

"Out of the sky."

"The *sky*?"

"I was in recon in the Marines. Dante is just a bat shit millionaire adrenaline junkie."

"You really do like to live dangerously."

"Yes, I do." When he swung his gaze back at her, it was thick, unwavering. So was his gait as he prowled back to her. At last, he nudged the ankle of her top leg with one foot. He pushed until she lowered it, resulting in her sitting in front of him, one of her calves captured by his legs. "Why do you look so surprised by that?"

She tried to straighten a little. He didn't yield the hold.

"I'm not surprised. It actually helps my case."

"And what case would that be, specifically?"

He gave up the lock on her leg—so he could shift his position, straddling her thighs. He curled forward, bracing both hands to the chair's arms, crashing through every inch of her physical space. The awareness of him, in every beat of her blood and inch of her skin, made her breathing spike, her skin burn, her senses swim. By some miracle, she managed to keep her eyes open. It bolstered her enough to attempt speech.

"Look, I'm not going to deny that we have an attraction..."

"And that's dangerous?" He fixated on her neck like Barnabas Collins after a dry spell.

"Y-Yes."

"Because?" He smirked when she only gulped hard. Brushed her hair off her bared shoulder. "I'm listening."

"Senator—"

"I prefer it when you call me Sir." He traced her collarbone with his thumb. His touch was rough, possessive. Her breath came in audible stammers. His eyes dilated. *Hell.* The expression transformed him from totally mesmerizing to fucking hot.

"I'm not the one you want for this. I wish I could be, but I'm just too—" She grabbed his hand, forcing him to stop and letting him behold her anguish. "I'm *not* the one you want, okay? Not by half. I'm not sophisticated, or graceful, or polished—"

"You really think that's what I want?"

"That's what you need, Senator."

She forced herself to emphasize the last word. Someone around here had to grow a chunk of logic. Apparently, it had to be her. Under other circumstances, she might've laughed at that. Placing herself in the same sentence as the word *logic*? Wow, the universe did have a sense of humor.

But the grandest joke would be continuing this. She had to keep remembering that—to recommit to her resolve. She was here to move forward, not revisit a past where passion had led to ruin. That included pushing on, even when his silence went into Freeze-button mode. "Look, I don't like it either," she stated. "But what you need is—"

He cut her short with a burst of vicious strength. Before she could get out a gasp, he flipped their grip, fully controlling the pressure now. His hands squeezed her shoulders with angry intent. "Don't tell me what I fucking need."

"I'm just trying—"

"*Don't* tell me what I need. I think I know the answer to that by now. Look at me. Now. Into my eyes, not at my chin." His gaze stabbed her, packed with a thousand golden spikes. "Who's crammed your head with the crap that you're not *enough*? Owen? Was that the dickwad's name?"

She tried to laugh. To her horror, tears brimmed instead. "No!"

"Then what was his name?"

Thank God for a chance to shake her head. "No, *no*. You've got the name right, but it wasn't Owen. He didn't..." She swiped her free hand across her cheek. "He never said a word. It wasn't him. It wasn't anyone, okay?"

"The hell it wasn't." He snared that hand too, interlocking his fingers to it and then pushing it against the chair, next to her ear. "Somebody filled your mind with the idiocy that you're somehow..." He stared deeper, looking like he couldn't believe the lunacy of his next word. "Broken."

"Damn it."

She didn't mean to sob both syllables. Yet as soon as they were out, the damn of emotion burst open. "Did you ever stop to think it's because I *am* broken?"

She should have torn her clothes off for him then and there. She'd be less exposed, less horrified, and battling less torture in her soul. *Broken.* It was the perfect word and the perfect torment at once. "Leave me alone," she sobbed, pushing against him. "Let me up. You're suffocating me. I'm serious. Please. I'm hot. *Hot.* Too hot."

To her shock, he complied. Rose tore up from the chair. She was sweating, trembling. Her nerves were a swarm of fire ants. Even her fingernails throbbed with heat.

Relief beckoned, steps away. In a haze, she kicked off her shoes and stumbled toward the pool. Her intention was a wade in along the first step, but she shook so badly she missed, tumbling in face-first. She only went under for two seconds, but the damage was done.

She popped up, drenched and humiliated. "*Shit.*"

The same word burst from Mark's lips as he sprang into motion, intensifying her horror. He bounded in, plowing through the water like it was simply air.

"What the hell are you doing?"

"*Not* what you want to ask right now." His retort was damn near a snarl. He came closer by the second, shirt clinging to the ridges of his pecs and abs, the water turning his beard dark gold.

"Are you crazy?"

"Also not the right thing to ask."

"I tripped, okay? But you—oh crap, your clothes!"

His stare dipped, going wildcat again as he beheld what the water did to her linen blouse against her bra-free breasts. "*Your* clothes."

"I'm not wearing thousand-dollar Cavallis."

He jerked off the shoes and his socks, hurling them into the deep end of the pool. "Stay on topic." He stepped close enough to grab her elbow. Hard. "Why the hell do you talk about yourself like this? Who have you let into your head, to paint these ass-backward ideas? I want my answer, Rose. Now."

She flung her other arm out, slamming water at him. "Ass-backward? Really? Do you need more evidence than the situation you're in, Mr. Moore? I'm impetuous. Ill disciplined. I say the wrong things. I do the wrong things." She managed to wrench from his hold but realized he gave her no place to go. Two steps back, and her waist hit the side of the pool. "Why do you think I try so hard at the Victorian priss thing? Because I'm not!"

"Thank God."

Hell. He sounded like he meant it.

Rose tried to get around him again. He was more than ready, snaking both arms out and locking in her shoulders. He slid a smile of victory. She shot him an open grimace.

"Fine. You want to know? For starters, I have too much mouth and not enough manners." It was easy to spit it out. God knew she'd heard it from Shane enough. "Let's see. What else? Too much sass, not enough poise. I'm too talkative, too opinionated, too outgoing and, apparently, much too passionate."

Not that her brother knew anything about passion—

which might not be such a shitty thing. At twenty-eight, Shane had already made partner in a major Chicago law firm, yet here *she* was, soaked in a swimming pool, makeup coursing her face, listing everything she'd done to royally derail her life—to a man who, foreseeably, wanted to make her his slave-girl kink bunny.

And battling a large chunk of her brain telling her to let him.

"No. Not too passionate." Unbelievably, the rage in his face deepened—but the anger was joined by something else. It looked a great deal like the expression he'd given her neck a few minutes ago, only hungrier. Much less willing to let her go, no matter how hot she got now.

"Really?" It was a feeble attempt to screech the brakes on her racing senses. "Then tell me what the hell I *am*."

By unnerving degrees, he pressed closer. When Rose was pinned between his body and the pool's edge, he shifted his grip from her hands to her wrists—using those elegant vises to push her arms to her sides.

"You're a creature, wild and beautiful, who just needs the right master to guide you. To hone that passion. To let it shine." He circled her arms back so her wrists rested on the pool's edge. He kept them there by securing both with one of his hands. He raised his other hand, urging her face back up with a firm sweep of fingers. "Every fiber of you wants it, don't you, pet? You've had desires...fantasies...haven't you? And Owen was the man you were going to marry, the man you longed to fulfill those dreams. So you went to him and opened up to him a little. Maybe a lot."

"Oh."

It was all she could say as his nearness turned their

proximity into incredible humidity. How did he know? How *could* he have known?

But he did. Somehow, he did.

"Yeah." He nodded, looking satisfied yet still plenty pissed. "That's exactly what happened, wasn't it? You went to him, you bared yourself to him, and the goddamn boy got so scared of having the passion of a real woman on his hands, he shit in his diapers and ran."

Despite the big beautiful nearness of him and the sparks flying between them at nearly visible intensity, she shivered. The disaster with Owen...she'd never heard it explained like that before. Could it be...maybe a little of it...wasn't her? Could it be she wasn't a complete disaster? Could it be that maybe, given the right place, the right man, all the secret yearnings of her heart and all the dark needs of her body...were okay?

But this wasn't the right place. This wasn't the right man. They were from different worlds, different life paths. At least with Owen, she had hope of being enough, squeezing enough into the mold. But this golden god, who stripped her of all rational thought? No. She'd disappoint. Would never be enough.

She'd come here tonight to tell him exactly that.

So tell him.

Her brain railed it at her drunk senses like a nagging designated driver. It kept trying even as he wrapped a hand to the back of her head, anchoring it in place to excavate her gaze with his. Then her bloodstream took over. It grabbed those keys of self-control and hurled them into the thickest bushes of her mind.

She was so in trouble now.

"I don't scare easily, Rose." His breath filled the air

between them, scented with Scotch and wind and desire. "I want your passion. I need your fire. This is good. This is right. *You're* so right." He dipped his head, brushing his lips along the seam of hers, sending a thousand more frissons through her body. "Give in to it, for just tonight. Give me the chance to show you how amazing it can be, how amazing *you* can be. Submit to me, pet. No obligations other than now. No thoughts beyond this."

He finished the promise by filling her mouth with his, taking her like a man possessed, slanting her back with voracious force. He swept her hard with his tongue, exploring her, claiming her. Rose moaned, fascinated by the contrasts surrounding her body, her senses. This hot, wet kiss. This cool, teasing water. This fluid, powerful man. His solid, searing touch. She yearned to get her hands on him in return, but his grip on her wrists tightened. She had to show him her heat and her need in other ways. She pushed her face higher, trying to suck his tongue in. She writhed and whimpered, now blatantly aware of the soaked fabric against her hard, achy nipples.

When he finally pulled away from her, a single word sighed up her throat.

"Yes."

A low sound of pleasure came from his throat. "Yes what, pet?"

"Yes, I... I'll submit to you. Sir."

"Oh, *honey.*" He kissed her again, brutal and fast. "You have no idea...what that does to me."

She grinned. "Oh, I have a little bit of an idea."

"Ssshh." Without taking his eyes off her, he lowered his hand, unbuckled his belt, and slid it off. The only sound between them was water dripping off the leather strip as he circled it behind her and then cinched it around her wrists in place of his other hand. She watched his face as he looped the strap back under, slipping the end between her wrists, rendering them immobile between her lower back and the pool's edge. His lips were parted, his jaw was set, his eyes were fires of fierce concentration. When he was finished, her elbows lay flat against the tile, their curves turned into little coves. As the water lapped at the sensitive skin there, every nerve ending on her arms shimmered in awakening.

He wrapped both hands to her back, running them over her bonds, testing to make sure she really couldn't move. His stare bore into hers again. "Too tight?"

"No, Sir." She whispered it, now entranced with his concentration on her. He focused with a heady mix of all business and pure lust. Nobody had ever looked at her like this.

He didn't miss the change in her voice either. He pressed her forearms firmly, declaring how he understood the enormity of her decision. He kept his grip firm despite her trembling, nostrils flaring as if just that little act aroused him.

"You're so breathtaking."

His words were heavy and rough. He lowered his head to her shoulder, teething her skin as he lifted a hand to her breast. His thumb swiped her nipple through the wet cotton. More electricity sizzled through her. Rose gasped and lurched toward him.

"Easy, Rose. It's okay. I'm going to take care of you, don't worry."

She tried to get air, but every breath pushed her breast into his hand again, inciting the need to be closer, to get more of him. Without thinking, she tugged against her restraint. Without thought, she cried out in frustration. "Easy? This isn't easy!"

He laughed—laughed!—and locked his other hand to her hip. "I need to know something."

She glowered against his chest. "The answer is yes."

"Yes?"

"Yes; I'm dying to get my hands on you."

He chuckled again. The sound was a maddening mix of warmth and desire. "That's not your place right now, pet." He ignored her little huff, which halted when he asked with seriousness, "I need to know...in those clubs you went to with your friends, did you learn about safe words?"

Her stomach clenched—though this time in a good way. "Yes, Sir."

"Then do you know what yours is now?" He pulled back, tilting his head in question. She was so deliciously smooth. So goddamn hot.

"Extemporization?" When his stare turned into a glower, she sighed. "Fine. Yes. My safe word is worth." She stuck in a mocking edge to her finish. "Sir."

He angled his face over hers now. His fingers closed tighter on her breast. "I shouldn't let you get away with that." He added a harsh tug to the ends of her wet hair. With her neck bared to him again, he nipped at the hollow of her throat and then the valley between her breasts. "I should rip this blouse off your shoulders and bite your sweet, hard nipples until they're red and sore. Yet still, my pet, you'll beg me to nibble them one more time, just so you can climax for me in a million throbbing pieces."

His voice wove its rough magic down, down, boldly gripping her sex.

"Yes," Rose pleaded. "Oh yes, please, Sir."

"No." He took a step back, slipping buttons out of his shirt to bare his hard, golden-skinned chest. "You're going to come with my cock buried deep inside you, honey. And you're going to feel beautiful as you do. Beautiful and sexy and very, very fulfilled."

With those soaked white panels now hanging off his bulging, broad shoulders, he delved his arms beneath the water and hiked her skirt to her waist. Once he got to her panties, he didn't bother tugging.

"In the way."

He hooked his forefingers to the elastic at both thighs and then ripped the thong free.

Through her lashes, Rose watched the lace float across the pool. It was an apt symbol of where her modesty, her logic, her determination, and her self-control had gone. As if she had a moment to mourn them.

"Eyes here, pet." Her gaze was commanded back up by Mark's fingers beneath her chin. "And do *not* close them. I want to see it all from you, every moment of it."

"Every moment...of what?"

"Of your transformation."

Dear God. The man had a way with words. And the way he scraped every syllable into her, like sensual sandpaper, leaving her mind exposed and her body writhing... Could it be possible? Could she be changed, if only for this magical sliver of time, into somebody celebrated for her fire and not shamed for her cheek? Guided into a place where she was wild yet tamed, freed yet harnessed, detonated yet not destructive? Her heart burst with the possibility of it. With the miracle he offered.

A transformation...

Indeed, she felt like a butterfly crawling at its chrysalis

as he scooped his feet to the inner arches of hers, spreading her legs with his, opening her core to the wet, hard press of his body. She sighed with the onslaught of sensations. The hard, pressing demand of his feet against her insoles. The cool kiss of the water on the hot folds of her sex. His control. Her vulnerability. Her breath came in urgent thrusts as she struggled to process it all but couldn't. Her head fell back. She slammed her eyes shut, needing the sanity of the darkness behind her lids.

"No." His reprimand was vicious this time, backed by one hand at her chin and the other at the top of her blouse. His shoulders bunched as he pulled the garment, exposing one of her breasts. He pulled her nipple with a long, hard pinch, making her glare. "No shutting me out." He bared his teeth, smiling like a mountain lion on the prowl. Great. She was a flitting pollinator; he was a nocturnal predator. Worst of all, her body reveled in the contrast. Her pulse fluttered faster, and her pussy raced to catch up.

"Right here, Rose." His breath mingled with hers as he seated himself against her sex. His erection was full and hard beneath his pants. "Look. Here. At. Me."

"Can't." She couldn't help it. Her eyelids drooped as her thighs burned and her buttocks convulsed. "It's so much. Too much!"

"Because you're thinking about it. Let it go. Give it to me. All of it." His tawny eyes swept every inch of her face. "Goddamn it, you're exquisite like this."

A sob escaped her. Not just because of his words. It was the mirror of his eyes as he gave them, as he reflected how incredible her passion could be. The trait for which she'd always felt most ashamed was now a diamond chiseled from the cavern of her soul, the one thing she longed to set free, to be resplendent in the light of his gaze.

"That's it." His lips curled up. His hand, dipping beneath the water again, left a sensual splash in its wake. "You remember last night?" he murmured, finding his way to the moist curls at her center, fingers exploring the soaked little forest. "You remember our little repetition exercise, Ms. Fabian?"

She shivered and whimpered. His penetration was steady and sure...and magical. Without her arms, all she could use for communication were her lips, which she used to nuzzle him, and her torso, urgently thrusting toward him. "Yes. Yes, Sir, I remember."

"Mmm. Good. So you remember your body is beautiful?"

"Yes!" She nodded as he shifted the hand at her breast, starting to massage the peak in an erotic circle.

"And your desire too? And your surrender?"

"Yes." He changed the torment of his lower hand, raking his fingers deeper, finding her most tender flesh. He coaxed the soft nub out, splintering her. "Yes! M-My desire too. And my...my..."

"Your surrender. Say it, honey. Just to me. Just *for* me."

"My...my surrender is beautiful." She offered it with panting need, jerking her hips and craving more of his touch. With every swipe, his fingers shot an arrow of heat into the most illicit tissues of her womb.

"Yes, it is—but you're not giving it to me yet."

"B-But I—"

"Need to be still, pet. You'll get what you need, but not if you're a moving target."

She groaned. Was he kidding? She clenched her thighs and tried to be good, to stay immobile. With an appreciative hum, he began the sensual pressure on her breast again. He started moving his fingers in her intimate folds as well...a dance of knowing, seductive spirals...

It was torment. It was heaven. Rose's blood turned to fire, raging hotter and faster.

"Oh," she finally cried, her mouth falling open. "Ohhh please!"

She couldn't believe the control in his face and the surety of his fingers. While he smiled with pleasure from her reaction, not one muscle shook in his body. He was maddening and mesmerizing. Completely in power. Totally in his element.

"We're going to add a new affirmation tonight." He said it as he tugged the other shoulder of her blouse down. "Are you ready?" Her newly revealed nipple slipped into his warm, consuming mouth. The tight bud tingled from his touch and sent ripples of new awareness through her whole body.

"I...I don't know what I am anymore."

It was the truth, and his knowing chuckle told her he knew it. His beard rasped the side of her breast, giving her delicious abrasiveness. "Give it to me nice and clear, honey. 'My passion is beautiful.'"

She would've complied, had he not picked that instant to intensify the strokes on her clit. He pulled her apart, strung her out, teased and nipped until she keened, acutely aware of the hot cream in her vagina, making her ready for more of him. "My—my—damn!"

Mark laughed again. It was better than a snarl of disapproval—*maybe*. If he tantalized her like this much longer, her whimpers would burst into something for the whole island's ears. "Oh yes, Rose. You're incredible. Look into my eyes and see yourself reflected there. See yourself as I see you.

Then give me the words. Give them to me and believe them."

The rough raffia of his tone was sweet bondage on her gaze, lifting her lids so she could take in the fire of his stare. And as he promised, she did see herself there. In the sheen of his lust, she saw an adorable and sexy pet. In the deeper shades beneath, she saw a woman desired, needed. And in the darkest labyrinths, nearly black in hue, she comprehended the most special beauty she held to him, the most precious gift she'd given him. She saw the breathtaking strength of a Dominant, at *his* fullest glory. He'd been transformed too.

As those comprehensions filled her, she longed to say the words for him. She needed to. And she meant every syllable of them as they emerged without a falter. "My passion is beautiful...Sir."

CHAPTER NINE

Mark knew she'd say it. He had no doubt she'd give him the words, even before he gave her the direction. He'd gotten the confirmation again when ordering her gaze into his and had made her behold the truth of all this: that despite her locked wrists and spread legs, she was still the one here with the power.

What he hadn't expected was how she'd bottle the strength into five words—and with the sweet gift of her voice alone, throw it all back at him. *Into* him.

The impact shoved the air from his chest.

"Christ."

He barely got it out. The enormity of her gift slammed him with every passing second, with every new emotion igniting the curves of her face. This woman's spirit had been trampled for so long, subjugated nearly her whole life. That Rose trusted him with it now, giving it over with such clarity and conviction, acted like a rainstorm on the mountainside of his self-control. The whole thing slid away in one sweep.

And what was left?

The granite cliff of his Dominant.

"Very good." He loved how the grit in his tone made her lashes fly up, her tongue dart out. "You *are* beautiful. And so hot and sweet." He tested her readiness by shifting two fingers into the tightness beneath her clit. Her walls sucked him in at once, a wet and pulsing heaven. His cock, already jammed against his fly, screamed at him for release.

He channeled the new tension into grabbing her under the ribs, lifting her out of the water, and parking her gorgeous backside onto the pool's edge. In one sweep, he hiked himself out too. She stared up at him with a little apprehension, but much of it disappeared as soon as he lifted her, cradling her close, before striding to a nearby chaise. After positioning her against the upright back of the chair, he took a moment to stand back and simply stare.

"Damn, I wish I had a camera." He lifted a long, appreciative smile. "But nobody would believe the picture was real. You're so fucking stunning like this, with the water dripping off you and your desire glowing from the inside out." He moved to the foot of the chaise, letting her watch as he pulled off his pants and briefs, setting his erection free. "See what you do to me?" With legs braced, he stroked himself, punctuating with a hiss from the sensual agony of it. His shaft stretched and grew as Rose arched her back, her breath quickening. "Now let me see what I do to you." It was a complete command, making her body tremble more and turning her nipples to pearls in the moonlight. "Lift your legs and spread them. One knee over each arm of the chair. Open yourself for me."

She gasped at that but in all the right ways. Holy fuck, he wasn't going to last much longer. He knew it the moment she complied with his order, yet he didn't want this to end. He wanted to string out every moment of the look on her face, the glistening desire from her pussy, this airtight connection between them, this power transfer he craved.

"Oh, Rose." The words came from his gut. "Look at you, bound and beautiful and ready. You *are* ready, aren't you? Your thighs are trembling, and your cunt is glistening." He raised his stare, taking in the gorgeous wince on her face. "What do you need, pet? I want to give you whatever you desire."

Her answer took barely two seconds. "You."

"Me?" He gave her a slow smirk. "Me...how?"

"Inside me. Please...Sir."

When he'd first arrived at the villa, the concierge showed him a poolside credenza filled with assorted guest amenities. He'd nearly chuckled at observing the shelf filled with a selection of sex essentials. Now he covered the distance to that cabinet in two steps, ripped the door open, and grabbed a foil packet off the shelf. By the time he pivoted and knelt on the chaise between Rose's legs, he had the condom out and ready.

"Well," he drawled, rolling the latex over his swollen, aching length. "What the pet needs, the Master gives."

"Yes." She choked on whatever else she had to say, the sound dissolving into a gorgeous moan as he edged the hot head of his cock into her welcoming channel.

After that push, he was lost too. In one slide, he sheathed himself as far as he could go—giving over his own surrender. He was a prisoner of her heat, her tightness, her precious pulses of passion. He growled with the rightness of it, their stares connecting deeper as their bodies did, taking and giving to each other with each stroke. He braced his hands beneath her hips, cupping her ass as he thrust faster, harder. A breeze kicked the air, mixing the scents of sea foam and frangipani into the tang of their lust-slick bodies. That was the poetic part. Other smells pushed at his self-control too. The wet leather of his belt. The water on her skin. And yes, that lingering chill to her breath betraying the fear she still gripped, far down in her psyche.

Now, with her body around him and her wide dark eyes pulling him, he understood more of that distress.

Maybe...

Rose had known all along.

Maybe she'd sensed, in that crazy female way, that if they explored even a spark of attraction, it would explode into this consuming fire...threatening to melt much more than their bodies...

But even as the thought terrorized his brain, he knew he'd never heed it.

With his gaze delving deeper into hers, he gritted one confirming word to that.

"More."

He dug his fingers into her soft skin, fully intending to leave marks.

"I need more, honey. Spread your legs wider. Tighten your muscles inside. Pull me deeper. *Deeper.* Take every inch, Rose!"

Her face twisted tight as she struggled to obey. It was a more stunning sight than any sunset this island could conjure. When she cried out from the extra depth he gained, he gritted his teeth in a pleased smile.

"Good," he murmured. "Very good. You're so good for me." As reward, he reached and loosened the belt, coaxing her arms forward. "Hang on tight, pet. This is going to be a great ride."

Her arms flung around his shoulders. The belt was still looped around one of her wrists, so the leather smacked his back with her motion. He groaned from the stinging bite of it. The breeze became gusts now. Water spanked the sides of the pool. He kept time, taking her so hard their bodies slapped. The smell of rain touched the air. Fitting. His senses were already a storm. He buried his face in Rose's neck, losing himself in her racing heartbeat, her tight body, and her panting, needing submission.

"Give it to me," he ordered into her ear. "Shatter for me, pet."

Two more thrusts, and she was a ball of thorough obedience. Her cry, high and keening, hit the air like lightning and his balls like wildfire. As she shuddered with her orgasm, her walls convulsing around him, the flames shot up his shaft. His orgasm hit in a wild, hard rush. Silver specks danced in his vision.

He couldn't think. For a second, that panicked him. He'd never been unable to keep control, to be aware of outside elements as he took a sub to completion, especially in a chaise lounge on an island resort with a spring storm approaching.

But Rose was no ordinary submissive.

Rose was no ordinary anything.

As equilibrium returned, he actually chuckled at the thought. The description had come upon him so easily, and he wasn't about to take back a word of it. Because it was all true.

Rose arched her neck, shuddering from the little movement of his mouth. "Holy. Shit." It came out on a pair of gasps. "Are you *laughing*? I can...barely...think."

He kissed the ridge beneath her ear. "Because you, my sweet, submissive girl, didn't just come out of the kinkster closet."

"Huh?"

"You tumbled."

She snorted. "I was pushed."

He moved his lips along her jaw, nibbling his way to her mouth. "We're at an impasse, hmm?" After giving her a swift kiss, he flashed an enigmatic smile. "Maybe we'll just need a do-over."

She turned her face, looking delectable even in her confusion. When she pressed the back of her hand to her forehead, he took the chance to run gentle fingers over her wrist. The skin was still scuffed but would likely clear up in a few hours. He pulled his fingers back, replacing them with his mouth. No kisses this time. He licked her skin instead. Yet as her breath jolted faster, spurring his tiny laves into broader swipes, fat raindrops began plopping on them.

"Pool party's over." He adjusted her blouse back into place. Trusting her skirt would drop down of its own accord when she stood—or maybe not, and that was all the better—he rose and yanked on his pants, barely zipping before he picked up his briefs and her shoes. "Come." He reached for her. When she hesitated, he quipped, "I'd make some excuse about not wanting you to get wet, but I have a hunch you'd see through me."

That thawed her quiet awkwardness. A little. As they walked into the villa, she replied, "It's perfect timing, anyhow. Now nobody will question the state of my clothes."

He stopped. "Why would anyone question your clothes?"

It was a rhetorical question. He practically read the answer in the glance she gave the door but was going to make her voice it anyhow. "It's not a short walk back to my room, Senator. And it's not too late yet. People will still be up. And—"

"And what if I kept you here until it *is* too late?"

He cupped her shoulder. She wrenched away. He allowed the rebuff, but if she thought he'd let her lunge out, dismissing what they'd just done like nothing more than a summer storm, the woman was delusional.

Her shoulders hunched as she crossed her arms. Her

whole bearing edged back toward watchful caution. Mark fought the craving to shake her. To knock free the bricks of those walls she was erecting before his eyes again.

She set free a resigned sigh. "Is this where you tell me we need to talk?"

He planted a wide stance behind her. Peeled off his shirt so when she glanced back—and he suspected she would—she'd have to confront him in nothing but his conviction and command. Devious? Yes. Necessary? Also affirmative. There were more ways to knock down her bricks than the obvious.

"We can get there by talking. Or any other means necessary."

"Get where?" She turned and gaped. "Errmmm...Sena—"

"Oh, no. Don't you go there. You're not hiding me behind the *Senator* thing. Not now." He closed on her by another step. "You're still dealing with me as a man, Rose. As Mark. As Sir. And you're dealing with yourself and what you've just discovered about yourself. No sweeping this under the rug. No pretending it didn't happen." He leaned in, pulling her arms apart now and holding them at her sides. "No forgetting how you came apart for me. How you flew. How we both did."

The energy of her sob filled the air before the sound of it. "Damn it! You don't understand!" Despite the dismissal, she gripped his forearms like driftwood in a flood. "I have to forget, okay? I can't fly. If I fly, I fall—and it'll hurt. And I won't be able to heal the damage this time. I won't be...able to..."

The tears took over her voice, and her pain took over his heart. He enveloped her hands in his own before sliding them around his neck—and swore, if he ever met the people responsible for this disgusting mental programming, he hoped it was in a crowd. In close quarters, the bridge between his rage and his fists wouldn't stay intact.

"You won't fall, sweetheart." He tucked her head into his chest. "I swear it. I won't let you."

She softened against him. She fit there so perfectly, smelling of rain and vanilla and sex...surrounding his senses.

Unchaining his soul.

"Rose," he whispered. "*Rosalind.* Sweet pet..." The last of it died in the beginning of their kiss, a consummation of tongues and lips and need. A mewl swirled up her throat, unfastening his self-restraint by a dozen more latches. He ended the kiss by twisting a hand into her hair. She hissed as her head arched back, a sound mixed of pain and pleasure, driving him to sink his teeth into the flawless column of her neck.

"Y-You have to s-stop calling me th-that," she stammered.

He went for the sleek line of her jugular. "Hmm. All right. If you really don't like it..."

"I love it." She tunneled her fingers into his hair. "Which is why you need to stop."

Dark growl. "That, my *pet*, is called topping from the bottom. And if you're not careful, it'll get you punished."

Her hands stilled against his scalp. She tugged her head back, catching his eyes with a look he'd not seen from her before. Her face quirked with mischief. She sucked in her bottom lip by a few coy degrees. "Punishment? For topping from *what* bottom? I'm not on the bottom."

He tossed his head back, laughing loud. "And that wasn't very careful!"

She smiled a little, getting ready to pop off a victorious giggle, until he flung her all the way over his shoulder.

"Aggghhh!"

He gripped her thigh with a savoring snarl. "Beautiful

scream. Give me another, honey. My ears don't care, but my cock's listening loud and clear."

"Damn it! Senator! Wait—*Owww*!"

Her howl came with the smack he dropped to the curve of her ass. "Call me Senator again, and it'll hurt twice as much. You were warned, Rose. As long as we're at it..." He added another spank. This one was less intense. "That's a reminder about the not-so-small attempt to top."

"I didn't know that's what it was!" Her protest was filled with genuine outrage. But her body conveyed another message. There wasn't an ounce of resistance in her muscles, even as he took her to the bedroom with purposeful strides.

"Right." He drew out the word in disbelief, just as Dante had an hour ago. He forced his face to convey the same thing as he flipped her over, tossing her to the center of the bed. It was damn hard to hold his scowl. She was so adorable. He gazed at her, damp and sputtering, her skirt nearly hiked to her waist again, giving him tantalizing peeks at her bare mound. She gaped at him, eyes burning with dark-bronze radiance.

"What the... I was just—"

"Wondering why you weren't on the bottom." He curled fists to his hips, standing at the foot of the bed. "Which fit perfectly with my own dilemma, wondering why you keep denying the magic of who you can be. So here you are, Rose."

She pushed up onto her elbows. Gave a moue of resignation. "On the bottom."

"On the bed," he clarified. "On the *bottom* comes next, unless you take the invitation now to get up and leave. The choice is still yours. But let me be clear. We're beyond talking about this, and I'm beyond chasing you. If you stay, you give up the choice to run from me, at least for tonight. If you stay, you're giving yourself—and your control—to me, for the entire night. If you stay, I'm going to do everything in my power to seduce you, command you, and fuck you into seeing the gift of who you are, what you want, what you need. I'm going to do it as many times as it takes until you believe me." He savored the disconcerted flutter of her lashes and the way her breathing intensified. "You'll sleep eventually because you need to for instruction tomorrow, but you'll do it at my side, in my arms. Everything clear?"

Her face showed a kaleidoscope of feelings as he finished the ultimatum. And yeah, ultimatum was the best way of putting it. Fuck subtlety. He was done with that, if they could even get away with the label for where they'd been so far. What they'd even tasted so far with each other was worth honesty in its most ruthless form. This woman...fed him. Satiated an awesome beast in him. And whether she accepted it or not, he'd awakened an answering animal in her too. He wanted more of *that* creature. He wanted to give *her* more. What she could discover beneath his touch...the fathoms of herself, of her beauty...*hell*. He was going to be hard-pressed to teach her all of it in the week they had left, but he was sure as hell willing to try.

But if he had to shove his beast down again, he needed to know now.

Otherwise, his Dom was going to break free completely— and enjoy a nice, extended stay in the magnificent landscape of Rose Fabian's mind, body, and soul.

CHAPTER TEN

Rose tried to look away. God, she needed some balance. Just a second of escape from the maelstrom of her senses, for which *he* was responsible. But her stare kept gravitating to him alone.

He reminded her of a caged, enraged lion. Yet his words had made things clear. *She* held the key to that cage. If she got up and walked out now, his confinement would remain intact. What had happened outside would remain a secret forever, for the two of them alone. A beautiful, inescapable memory. A night she'd undoubtedly play over and over for the rest of her life, remembering the man who'd seen into the untamed depths of her soul, shone his golden gaze on it, and made her feel, for once...

Perfect.

The word became a taunt in her head as she fell to the coverlet, throwing both arms over her face.

Why the hell had she given in? Why had she even come here tonight? Why, damn it, had he given her a taste of perfect, knowing she couldn't choose more for all the most right, sane reasons—

Knowing she'd throw them all away to get just one more bite.

She balled her hands, swiped them across her stinging eyes, and rose to a sitting position. She tucked both legs beneath the ass still stinging from his whacks.

"I'm scared."

"I know."

Mark's voice, full of gravel and command, brought back how he'd made her feel out by the pool. Drenched in his power. Lost in his control. Reveling in the open flood of his lust. And yes, even loving how he'd bound her. Ohhhh, yeah. Loving that part the most. In confusing, terrifying, I'm-going-to-lose-myself-completely ways.

Now she was really scared.

The conclusion beat harder into her blood as he climbed onto the bed too. Rose swallowed. Were his thighs always built like a racehorse, or was she noticing now because he flexed them with such authority?

He pulled her up so their kneeling poses matched. He kept his hands on her shoulders, kneading her skin with deep, assessing strokes. "You're trembling."

"Y-Yeah."

"Are you cold?"

She pulled in a breath. His scent filled her head, wild and wet, like the storm gathering force outside. "No."

He inhaled too. Trailed his fingertips down her arms, stopping at her wrists. "It turns me on."

His voice was a serration of sound, sending quivers into the extremes of her body. When she raised her gaze over the balanced ridges of his abdomen, she stopped at the solid planes of his pecs. His nipples were rock hard.

She shivered again.

His fingers tightened on her wrists. Then circled both of them. "Is this scary?"

She looked down to where he clasped her. His long, strong fingers were dark-gold shackles around her lighter skin. "A little."

"Enough to stop?"

"*No.*" The force of her protest came as a surprise. She shot her gaze up to his, knowing she likely looked like a fool, though she couldn't stop. He fixated her, the complete combination of everything that was right and wrong, like looking at the sun without eye gear. What a beautiful way to burn out her senses.

"Please," she implored. "Don't make me keep thinking about this. Don't make me keep choosing."

"Not an option." His eyes darkened to amber embers. "You have to choose, Rose. You need to. I want to dominate you, not force you."

The way his voice dropped on that sentence, dipping each syllable in thick, sensual intention, coated her whole body like melted butter. She flashed her tongue out, as if needing to taste the stuff too. And was unable to fight the temptation anymore.

"And if you were dominating me right now, what would you do?"

A sound between a rumble and a hum vibrated from his throat. Five seconds later, he snared both her wrists in one of his hands, jerked them high over her head, and used that leverage to shove her down to the bed. As he followed her down, he shoved the insides of her thighs with the outside of his own. Inside another five seconds, she was captive and spread for him.

And instantly wet for him.

His gaze dropped, skating over her nose and then down to her mouth with hungry intent. Her lungs ached in response. She couldn't get enough air. And she never wanted to again.

"I'd probably do something like this," he murmured. "And then something like...this."

He took her lips then, going slow and sensuous for all of

two seconds. More than fine with her. She couldn't take the love-me-tender approach for longer than that. She purposely drove him on with a moan bordering on protest, knowing what his mouth was capable of inciting in her now—and craving more.

Lightning sizzled the air with electric heat.

She sucked his tongue hard, a negative charge needing its positive.

Mark's hand corkscrewed around her wrists. With his other hand, he pulled her chin down, opening her wider for the stabbing invasion of his mouth. Their noses slammed. Their breaths mingled. They tore and tugged and bit at each other. She couldn't get enough of him.

Not...

Enough...

Thunder boomed through the room, as if the universe confirmed what she already knew. The switch of hesitation had been flipped. No turning back now. No wanting to. No needing anything except how this man ignited her.

They finally pulled back from each other with protesting groans. She stared in fascination as Mark released her and reared up. Veins stood out against the muscles of his torso. His mouth was parted; his teeth were bared. He was a living embodiment of untamed lust...and her deepest fantasies.

Three words came out of him with hard command.

"Strip. Everything. Now."

He shoved back to give her room. Rose still trembled but obeyed. The blouse was the easy part since he'd already taken advantage of its design tonight. When she lifted to her knees to slide off the skirt...that was when her hesitation sneaked in. She wasn't naive. She kept some of the jiggle in check with a jogging addiction, but her backside wasn't ever going to grace a swimwear runway. Okay, so he'd seen the goods before—but what happened in the fitness room seemed an accident, a dream. This was more real. More significant. More of what it was. A choice. A huge one.

"Rose." His husky murmur came as soon as she slipped the skirt to the floor. "You're so fucking stunning."

She attempted a smile. She was totally unsure how to respond, what to do. His stare burned every inch it scanned, making her even more aware of her nakedness, paralyzing her with its heat.

"Stay right there, pet. Spread your knees just a little more and get your balance."

So much for wondering what to do. Only now, thanks to his unfaltering tone, she actually felt the cream of her pussy drenching her folds as she complied. She couldn't help but roll her hips, gasping with her growing arousal.

"Very nice, honey. But let's not get ahead of ourselves. Lace your fingers together behind your head. Straighten your spine. Show me those beautiful breasts. Don't ever be ashamed of your body when you're with me."

"When you're with me." The words sang through her senses as she moved into position. The statement and the way he'd said it with such surety...they implied things, didn't they? Like maybe there'd be more nights like this. That this was just the first of many things he wanted—no, expected—her to remember when they were together. Even the consideration of such a thing filled her with a joy as she spread wider for him, uncovering her heart, just a little bit more, just as she bared her body.

Mark easily closed the distance between them. He spread

his fingers, raking the tips up her stomach, ribs, and then higher. Rose's breath hitched. Her pulse spiked. She shook again as he curled a slow smile. Once his hands were at her breasts, he cupped them possessively. The swells rose and fell against his fingers as he tugged her nipples to attention, playing along their hard plateaus with little scrapes of his thumbs.

Her sigh became a gasp of desire—and amazement. She'd experimented a few times with touching her breasts but had no idea they could feel like this. She'd never thought a knowing tease on her nipples would have repercussions deep in her womb, igniting her with waves of such exquisite pleasure. It was beautiful. Wonderful.

Magic.

"Time to wake her up completely, Rose." He said it as he pinched her tips even tighter.

"W-Wake who u-up?"

"You already know. *Her.* The Rose inside you. The one who's wanted this...who's yearned to be at the mercy of a man, to feel him pushing you like this. Demanding more from you like this."

As he drew the last word out with carnal languor, he turned his fingers into dual clamps, squeezing the tips of her breasts without mercy. In an instant, taunting pleasure became shooting pain.

"Shit!" She dropped her hands and shoved at him. Why her pussy pulsed harder, she had no damn idea.

Mark narrowed his glare. Tilted his head.

Doubled the pressure on her nipples.

Rose keened.

Then glared.

"Get those hands back up behind your head, pet. I won't ask again."

She had no idea why she complied. But something deep in his voice spoke to the darkest chemistry of her body, driving her arms back up. She shook from the confusion. "What the hell is wrong with me?" she pleaded. "This is wrong! I shouldn't want this!"

"Really?" The man had the nerve to smile as if she'd simply admitted a craving for peanut butter and pickle sandwiches. Without saying another word, he released his hold and then slid off the bed and stood behind her. He pressed close, reaching to cup a hand over the tight curls that shielded her sex. With knowing confidence, he wove two fingers through her slippery tissues—but didn't stop there. He twisted his wrist, working his long digits inside, chuckling in response to her gasps. "Your body tells me differently, Rose. Fuck, you feel so good. So tight and wet again."

He shifted closer. His breath became a harsh but warm wind along her back. It was barely a hint of the fire he delivered next. With his free hand, he gave a quick smack to one side of her ass. Rose cried out from surprise more than anything, softening to a sigh when he soothed the sting into sweet, arousing flames. After he did the same thing to the other side, she started writhing in need, grinding herself on the fingers still exploring her deep tunnel.

"Your body's screaming at me again, honey. You're soaking me. Clenching me." He sidled closer, pressing his hot, slick torso against her. "You don't just want this. You need it. You love that moment when the pain becomes fire, when the resistance turns into acceptance. When you know you've taken it, absorbed it, are stronger because of it. And you *are* strong, my Rose. So resilient and radiant. You captivate me with the strength of your surrender."

His words. His tone. His touch. It was an onslaught of adoration she'd never experienced from anyone. It was exactly what he'd promised. Transformation. Rose sagged beneath him, the last clouds of her resistance turned into the rain of her tears. She unclasped her hands from her head and roped them around his neck instead. She needed him close. Yearned to meld him and the truth he spoke into her heart forever.

"Yes," she said on a bare breath. "Yes...Sir...please..."

His beard scrubbed the top of her shoulder. "Please what?" he prompted. "Tell me what you need, honey. I'll give it to you. Anything."

She swallowed. Could she really do it? Really ask for the very thing she'd shunned from herself for so long?

But the alternative—a life without it—was now a worse thought to bear.

"More." It fell from her like a dead branch being cut off her psyche, freeing her soul, galvanizing her body. "More." She sobbed harder, pushing her backside at him to stress her meaning.

Aside from a thick breath, Mark didn't answer. He didn't have to. She knew he'd heard and understood. He proved it by dragging strong, sure fingers along the first ass cheek he'd spanked—and then slapping it again. The stroke was firm and steady, just like the flowing caresses that followed. He repeated the treatment to her other cheek. She gave a long sigh of thanks, thinking of all his words as the pain evaporated into warm steam along her skin.

You've taken it, absorbed it, it, are stronger because of it.

Yet she wanted more. No, not that. Mark had pegged it right, hadn't he?

She needed it.

"Again." The entreaty didn't even sound like part of her yet had never felt more intimate to her soul. "Please. Again. Harder."

Smack.

The impact of his flesh to hers reverberated in the room, a whip of sound against the sough of the rain. She released a moan, struggling to process how her body rebelled against this but her spirit reached so greedily for it.

Smack.

"Oh God!" Both sides of her ass prickled from the contact— yet she still needed more. Still craved to know what *more* felt like. Still longed to discover the parts of herself that could take it and what her body would do with the victory. "Please..."

He slid his hands to her nipples again. As he tugged both buds, he added on a stern direction. "No more words, pet. I'll give you what you need. Your submission is now to focus on my words and on what I've told you. Absorb them. Make them part of you and then give their power back to me with your entire body."

Yes, Sir.

She gave it to him with her soul as he delivered tougher spanks, this time to both sides of her ass at once.

"Good girl. Now lean forward." His voice was low and precise, claiming her will. "Your head on the bed. Your arms and hands stretched flat over it. Don't shift from that position, or I *will* find a way to bind you."

Thank you, Sir.

She threaded it through her sigh as she shifted into the position and then endured the stings of his next two slaps. They were even harder. Louder.

And yes...even more arousing as the pain dissipated...

swirling into tight tingles along her skin...

Please, Sir!

She punched it into the falsetto of her scream after his next two strikes. The impact shook her, forcing her to twist her hands into the bedcover. Mark barely massaged away the pain before dealing it again, a groan erupting from him now. His voice was a deep, feral creature, curling into her as he ordered her to breathe, to accept, to endure. And God, how she wanted to. There was no way to ignore her body's flooding need for more. Her blood raced, centering into her core. Her pussy clamped, making her yearn and burn and need him.

"Fuck. My sweet pet. So perfect."

Her world tilted. Her mind spun. His swirling, sweeping touch was magic on her enflamed backside before teasing into the valley between her thighs with his long, sure fingers. She rolled her hips, needing him deeper, harder. Her throat convulsed and let out a catlike cry as she struggled to hold her pleas in check.

"Fuck!"

After he growled it, the air was torn with the scrape of his zipper coming down.

"I'm nearly exploding, Rose."

He groaned again. The sound layered over a discernible crinkle of foil—and then his thighs were pressing against hers and his steel-hard, latex-covered shaft parted her from behind.

"I'm going to fuck you like this, honey. Dig in and hang on, because I'm going to give you more of what you need, I promise. Prepare your pussy. And your ass."

He was a man of his word. The moment the head of his cock connected to the depths of her sex, he squeezed her right ass cheek and then smacked it, solid and swift. With his left hand, he gave alternate strokes to the other cheek. It was agony, glory, sanity, and senselessness all at once, and she never wanted it to end. Clear thought? Forget it. Her body was in command now. No. *He* was in command now. He filled her. Consumed her. As his cock conquered her from the inside, his touch overpowered her from the outside. He was everywhere, bringing the intensity, the fever, the *more* for which she'd yearned her whole life. The experience she'd given up on ever having. The man she never thought she'd find. Who knew that flying to an island would really bring her an unexpected treasure?

Her world became a blissful mist as his thrusts took over her body. God, how she prayed the nirvana would last forever. The storm would rage on, the clock would stand still, the world would be simply this. Every cell in her body opened for him. Reached for him. Convulsed on waves that intensified with each passing second. Mindless sounds spilled from her lips as the sensations crashed in, faster and faster, falling on her like pulsing, pounding rain. And the storm kept flooding, slamming at the dam between sanity and mindlessness.

It wasn't long before fissures grew in that dam, wider and wider, promising to burst her open. She panted with need for it. She was going to burst. She was going to—

"Not yet, Rose. Hold it back. Let it grow a little more."

Was he kidding? "C-Can't! Too much! So...much!"

"Yes, you can. Not. Yet."

"Please!"

He spanked her with fierce, passionate force. "You're mine tonight. Your body is mine. Your orgasm is mine. Hold it back, damn it."

"Shit!" She gripped the bedcover so hard, she wondered

why the thing wasn't in shreds. "I hate you."

"I adore you." He relented his hold on her thighs, scraping forward to clutch her waist, forcing her body back onto his like they were gears on a locomotive. "Christ. I love fucking you."

The cracks in her composure split even more. "Please," she cried. "Oh please, Sir. I need to—"

"Yes." *Finally* the word she craved, needed. "Yes, honey. Come now. Come for me good!"

Good was just the beginning of what her detonation felt like. *Amazing* barely did it justice. If her brain was still functioning, it might've seized something like *volcanic*. She was a shifted landscape, an opened vista, the terrain of her psyche heaved up and turned into something new as she dissolved into raw sensation, pure light, magnificent heat, convulsing pleasure. She was exposed to him in ways having nothing to do with surrendering her body. This was about more, in so many precious ways. He'd known that. Oh God, how he'd known.

The sobs came again, taking over as he halted at the apex of a thrust. He shuddered. His cock tightened. He erupted hard and deep inside her. She felt the heat of his seed even through the latex sheath.

"Rose! Yes!"

It was the last thing he said for many long minutes. He drove into her with insatiable, athletic grace. She dissolved even more, yearning for the mist of mindlessness to go on forever...at the same time, bracing herself for the moment it didn't.

That instant came faster than she expected. And ten times worse than what she'd prepared for.

If her mind tumbled over a cliff before, it careened into a pit now. Everything was black, without direction, a no-man's land between the beauty of what they'd just shared and the confusion of why she saw it that way. What had she just done? What had she allowed *him* to do? And worse, why did it turn her inside out like nothing before, made her feel alive, afire, and perfect for the first time in her life?

Worst of all, how would she face a future of never knowing it again?

The truth plunged her deeper into the blackness.

Her sobs careened into nonstop weeping.

It took Mark less than a minute to pull out and lie down next to her. He reached for her with one hand while getting rid of the condom with his other. When that was done, he rolled to his back, his body coated in a sheen that looked too damn gorgeous for sweat, and then pulled her atop him. Rose burrowed close despite how a voice screamed from inside, telling her to get as far away as the bed allowed.

She needed to raise the shields again. She needed to start now. She had to chase down the emotional sentry who'd gone running with Mark's sensual invasion, sitting back to watch the show with amusement while her body and mind surrendered to his rule. If she got everything back in place now, maybe the damage to her composure could still be saved a little.

She wasn't fast enough. The shivers began anew. Every muscle in her body fell into paralysis. Mark stroked her temple, scraping back her hair with nurturing motions that tore open her emotional floodgates again. Within a few minutes, she'd soaked his chest with her salty storm.

"Crap." She finally raised her head and sniffled. "I'm a mess."

"You're supposed to be." He tucked her head back into his shoulder. "It's your first sub drop, honey."

She frowned. "Sub what?"

"Sub drop," he repeated. "Kink shorthand for a real biological sequence. Your body and your mind have been on high steam for over an hour. And after the release valve finally got punched..." His tone warmed with the innuendo. "Well, there was nowhere for you to go but down."

"Hm." The explanation made complete sense. But it didn't make the plummet any easier to endure. She closed her eyes in bliss as he started the finger-combing treatment again.

"Many submissives don't ever get used to it," he continued. "And if you don't either, that's okay too. We'll just make sure you're in a comfy place to fall every time."

His hand never stopped, but Rose's breathing hitched. There he went again, using those kinds of phrases. Stacking words and tones into a mental bridge that led to tomorrow, to the next day, to the next week, and beyond.

Weeks and months and tomorrows that could never be.

They'd be more than half a world apart by this time next month—but that was just the start of the problems. They already lived in different universes, and nothing would change that. He needed a woman to fly in the stars of his realm. He needed a companion who knew what do at his side in public as well as at his feet in private. Most of all, he deserved a woman who could give him her heart and soul as well as her body.

But wasn't that what you just did, Ro?

She trembled harder, as the answer to that resonated through her.

Yes, damn it. Yes. And it was the best experience of your life.

It was also the last time she'd let it happen. The last time either of them could let it happen.

Surely Mark saw that too. He wasn't a stupid man. But he

was also a determined, exasperating dreamer. His idealism was one of the most famous traits of his character. Until now, she'd always thought the media had just blown it out of proportion. Now she realized their accounts might have been exercising restraint.

A sigh spilled from her.

Mark's hand stilled against her head. "What is it, honey?"

She gazed at her fingers, lightly resting against his pec. "Please stop doing that." Before he could get in a note of protest, she went on. "You know what I'm talking about. We can't think about *every time* between us. There shouldn't have been a *this* time." She nuzzled his skin, breathing in the wild, masculine scent of him. "But I'm glad there was. Thank you."

His tense silence was broken only by the pattering rain. Finally he said, in a tight-teethed mutter, "We're not going to talk about this right now."

"That won't make it go away, Mark. Or our lives, or what—"

"Go to sleep, Rose."

"But you're just shoving it under the rug, damn it, and—"

"*Go to sleep*, Rose."

She turned the sigh into a huff. But after that, she said nothing. Weariness became a heavier blanket by the second, and morning was coming, as it always did.

In the light of day, he'd have to look at things differently. In a few hours, the world would be real again. Until then, she'd let herself believe his fantasy. A little while longer wouldn't hurt. She'd let herself be the transformed cinder girl and linger at the ball just a few minutes more—especially because this dance wasn't going to end with a glass slipper and carriage ride back to the palace.

After tonight, she had the rest of her life to remember that sometimes, pumpkins just had to remain pumpkins. It wasn't physically possible to turn them into princesses, and making them into pie only meant the prince ate them up before he decided they weren't the right flavor after all.

CHAPTER ELEVEN

The exhaustion of the sub drop claimed her within minutes. She didn't even rouse when Mark slipped from bed to grab a washcloth, soak it with cold water, and press it to the light welts he'd left on her ass. He cursed himself for not being more prepared with at least a cream for her skin, but that also had him admitting he'd never expected things to go as far as they had. He'd known he wanted to take her, to be inside her, to command her in every way he could, but he would've banked on a snowstorm hitting the island before predicting how deeply Rose would surrender to his hand...or how gorgeous she'd be in doing so.

How fully she'd blossom.

How completely she'd embrace it all.

How beautiful she'd be...in her submissiveness.

But she still didn't get it.

She'd ditched every lesson she'd just learned. She still thought this was a part of herself to be filed away like last year's tax return, not a vital element she'd never be able to forget again.

Foolish, frightened, stubborn...*incredible*...woman.

The litany rolled through his head, which now rested on the pillow next to hers. She was still lost to slumber, mahogany lashes fanned against her creamy skin, tangled hair dappled in the silver of the dawn. He swallowed as quietly as he could, studying her face, which seemed carefully composed even in her dreams. If she allowed herself to dream.

She challenged him in ways he'd never expected.

And she was worth every exasperating moment.

Rose sighed and stirred.

He smiled tenderly as his subbie stretched like a cat, throwing her arms over her head. The action tugged the covers off her chest, giving him an eyeful of her generous swells. His mouth literally watered as he took in the dusky areolae with their prizes so pert in the centers. He longed to lean over and coax both nipples into submission, but he held back. He figured once the air hit her bare skin, she'd—

"Shit!"

Bolt up and gape at him like that.

He bent an elbow and rested his head on his hand. If he didn't smile too broadly, maybe she'd keep neglecting to take the sheet with her. "Hi."

"Uh, hi."

Damn. She remembered. Dragged up the sheet, tugging her knees up too. With her free hand, she scraped back her hair. "I forgot where I was."

"You weren't looking too upset about it, sleeping beauty." At her humorless laugh, he probed, "What?"

She shook her head, seeming nervous. "Last night before I fell asleep, I was actually thinking—well, feeling—more like Cinderella."

Most women invoked that fairy tale with breathless glee. Instead, the sad threads in her tone made his chest tighten. "Sooty Cinderella or sparkling Cinderella?"

"A little of each, I guess. Loving the sparkle but knowing I'd have to wake up soon."

He'd expected that. But that didn't make it less maddening to hear. "No." He hooked a hand into the crook of her elbow, gripping harder when she tried to pull away. "Damn it, Rose. You *are* awake."

At last she looked at him. Her stare burned with a thousand questions but, most importantly, a little hope.

"Yes," he repeated. "Don't you see? For the first time in your life, you've accepted who you are. Submitting to me didn't make you weaker, honey. It gave you back your strength." He lifted his hand to her face, palming her jaw. "And it gave me back mine too. And I'm so thankful."

Her skin trembled beneath his touch. Her features contorted as if a boulder had landed on her shoulders. He watched every inch of her conflict, of the crossroads at which she stood. The safe comfort of yesterday's Rose, or the exhilarating terror of today's Rose?

Damn it. He refused to let her revert to the cinders. The past wasn't an option—for either of them.

"Mark," she whispered. "Please."

"*Rosalind.*" He flattened her torso against the fabric headboard. With the motion, he also rolled to crouch in front of her, cupping her cheeks. "Choose the strength. Choose this. Choose how good this can be."

Her gaze searched into him, big and vulnerable. But in those velvet depths, little rips of hesitation showed. Behind those rips, there was light...more glimmers...a little more anticipation.

She swallowed.

He held his breath.

Her chin quavered. But then she gave him a rasp that spun his hope into euphoria. "I can't!"

"You *can.*"

"Help me. No, *make* me. Please..."

It was all he needed to hear. He mashed his mouth to hers, not using a shred of gentleness about it. He sucked in her sweet taste, rejoicing in her plaintive mewl, hardening at her aroused shudder. *Fuck yes.* This was so right, and every cell in his being confirmed it. He stabbed his tongue to hers again and again, marveling at how she synched herself with his rhythm, at how perfect her hands felt around his neck, clawing his scalp. Heat thickened the air between them, turning the bunched sheets into an infuriating barrier. Like a man with a fever, Mark ripped them away. Not a far-flung comparison. Rose Fabian had infected his blood like a jungle virus, and he never wanted an antidote.

He dipped both hands between her thighs, parting them with one shove. Rose gasped, her tongue slipping along her bottom lip. In an instant he envisioned the length of his cock sliding into her berry-colored mouth. It turned his next words from a firm command into a raw growl.

"I'm not taking my time with this, honey. Listen close. The safe word is *worth*. Use it if you need to, but only if you *need* to. You've turned your will over to me. I won't abuse that, but I *will* push it. You need to be willing. And if you're willing, then you'll be obedient. Do you understand?"

He was mesmerized with how that affected her. The increased surges of her breath. The slight tilt of her head, leaning toward him, as if hungering for him.

"Yes," she finally blurted. "Yes, Sir, I understand."

He pushed forward to kiss her again. "Good girl."

A smile curved her lips. He took one second to bask in the adoring look before he swung off the bed, moving across the room with military efficiency.

"Sir? Wh-Where—"

"Questions will be kept to a minimum, Rose."

He kept his voice at a firm directive. A glance back showed him her reactions. Her hips writhed. Her gaze darkened. Her nipples were stiff points of attention. Quickly he moved to the gift basket GRI had sent to the suite. Damn thing could've carried Moses *and* a dozen cousins up the Nile. There was an equally large raffia bow on top of the package. He pulled the decoration apart until he'd unraveled the strong ribbon into two long lengths. A plan unfurled in his mind, filled with ruthless sensual intent.

He tilted a calculating grin at her. "You asked me to make you choose. Now trust that's what I'm going to do and don't doubt the process."

He scooped his necktie off the floor as he returned to the bed and then slid back to the mattress as he had last night. He balanced high on his knees, staring down at her flushed beauty. Her skin was cream and softness against the sheets. Her hair, rich and russet, tumbled against the headboard and around her shoulders. Her fathomless, long-lashed gaze never left him. Still he asked her, "Do you trust me, pet?"

Rose nodded slowly. "Y-Yes."

"It pleases me to hear that." He let her see his approving nod. "In that case, spread your legs wider for me."

She was a little shaky in her compliance. He clenched his jaw, struggling to forget the fresh rush of blood to his cock.

"Now move your wrists to the outsides of your knees." *Hell.* His erection jutted in front of him, prominent as Pinocchio's nose. "Perfect, honey. That's so damn perfect."

Without another word, he came forward to fasten her forearms to her lower thighs, twisting the raffia in a modified gauntlet pattern. The work was as gorgeous as it was practical. The knots were lined up in two neat rows but could be unraveled with one pull at the bows he secured at her wrists.

As he created the bonds, Mark's mind stepped into a place it hadn't been in years: a sacred corridor traversed only by Dom and sub together, tying up more than just body parts. A place where their breathing aligned and their awareness tunneled, where their heartbeats sought each other and the rest of the world got bound away as tightly as they were bound in. He truly never thought he'd know this precious silence again. Never thought he'd be using his strongest self-control techniques to keep an erection in check as he checked knots or be so focused on the answering signals from his submissive's body in return, tuning his senses so completely to her that he could take her pulse almost by looking at her.

And look he did. Hot and intent, over every inch.

"So beautiful," he murmured at last.

Rose returned a soft smile and a hooded gaze, her muscles taut but not strained, her desire showing in every shiny drop glistening along her open, sweet cunt. He bent to taste that delicious dew. She was so fucking sweet and creamy. She gasped, and he rose again to steal the sound with his open mouth.

Once he pulled away, he took the pinstriped tie. Stretched it in front of her face. As he expected, that keen mind of hers instantly understood his intent. Her breasts rose and fell in triple time. She blinked at the tie, clearly frightened but transfixed. Mark lightly scratched the back of her hand, forcing her to refocus on him.

"This is necessary, pet. Bondage and blindness. It means I get all your surrender now, in every way. I need it, and so do you."

Her face tightened, though finally she seemed to accept

his decision. He already had her splayed wide open but was now ordering her to stay that vulnerable to him—even as he plunged her into complete darkness.

Her total reliance on him.

His complete control over her.

Fuck, he needed this.

And whether she realized it fully yet or not...so did she.

He reached and wrapped the tie over her eyes.

He doubled the silk length back on itself, congratulating himself for picking the deep burgundy color. Maybe even back home, destiny had known how the hue would augment the classic coloring of the woman who'd open his world again. He didn't have a camera, so he indulged himself in a greedy gaze over every inch of her bound glory. After looking his fill, he brushed kisses to her forehead, the tip of her nose, and the planes of both cheeks. At last he took her lush mouth in a dominating kiss.

She opened for him with equal need, whimpering deeply, offering her tongue. His blood roared. His balls bellowed. They didn't waste time broadcasting their demand to his sex either. It was a riot from his sac to his helmet, seeped now with the heat of his pre-come. He groaned hard against her lips, needing to be inside her. Buried. Consumed.

Soon. *Soon.* After she was desperate too. After she begged for it.

"Let it go." He rasped it, letting Rose hear every note of her effect on him. "I'm right here, honey. You have nothing to worry about, nothing to control anymore. It's all mine, and it's safe. Your only task now is to feel."

He showed her what he meant by targeting the most sensitive parts of her body first. He dipped two moist kisses to the crevices behind her ears. He suckled two more to the skin just inside her armpits and another to the hollow of her neck. He moved lower, fingering her delicate navel, grazing his nails along her inner thighs, kissing the insides of her knees. He worshiped her toes, licking the nails with their rebellious gemstones, sucking on them with tender, taunting care. By the time he slid back up to capture her dark-raspberry nipples with his mouth, she struggled against her bondage and emitted bone-melting little cries. They escalated into miniature screams when he moved to the flesh of her breasts, tasting the skin in huge bites, even as his face dipped into the valley between the gorgeous globes.

"Ohhh, Sir!" She moaned as he kneaded both sides of her labia, using tiny circles to milk her clit, rushing the blood to her pussy and turning it into a rose of a hundred gorgeous hues. Mark hungrily looked his fill, adding light swats to the area with his fingertips. The beautiful wince on her face sucked the air from his lungs. He shook his head, completely amazed. How had this glorious woman ever thought she wasn't created for the magic of submission?

He moved his hand toward the tight channel of her sex. He went in with one finger, soon two, biting back his growl as her muscles clamped him in delicious welcome. He stretched in a third finger, reveling in the moisture now glistening in her folds. She threw her head back against the headboard, little sobs spilling up her throat. His ears heard every note—and his cock pounded with the echoes.

"Perfect, honey. So damn perfect."

He was transported as he gazed at her. The blindfold was a slash of sin across her face. Every curve of her body was flushed, wet, and ready for him. He slipped his fingers in and out, fucking her faster and faster with them. He thrusted and twisted, making her shake and gasp.

"Sir!" she pleaded. "Please!"

"Please what? Tell me what you're feeling, pet. Tell me what I can do for you."

"More! Please, just more!"

"More of what? Focus your thoughts. Tell me how it feels, honey."

"I...I...aaahhh!"

Her shriek came as he shifted his thumb, pressing it to the most sensitive ridge of her sex. He gritted his teeth, an action of his triumph and his struggle. He was soaring, high on being the one to make her feel this way, to open her up in this exquisite adventure of her sexuality and her soul—but doing it resulted in the most agonizing erection of his life. He glanced down at the angry red length with a silent promise.

Soon. Very soon.

"Talk to me, Rose." His efforts at control turned his syllables into bites. "Tell me what I do to you. I'm not asking. I'm commanding. Tell. Me."

She pounded her head back again, as if giving herself grounding for the task. He watched her brow furrow over the top of the blindfold.

"Heat," she finally blurted. "And...pressure. Wonderful pressure. And aching. Oh God, I *ache.*"

"Yes." Damn, she was so exquisite. So breathtaking in every moment she freed herself a little more. "Ache for what? Say it, honey."

"You. Please. Inside me. *Please!*"

It was all the invitation he needed.

Though he pulled his fingers free, Mark kept that hand

braced at her soaking folds, ensuring her entrance stayed spread and ready. He reached for the nightstand drawer, hoping it was as well stocked as the cabinet by the pool. Pay dirt. A neat stack of foil squares waited. He tore the condom wrapper with his teeth and sheathed up in seconds, clenching his jaw against the raw torture of it before pressing his whole body into her, locking his lips to her ear.

"I'm going to fuck you now, little subbie. Take me deep. Take me hard."

He dragged his lips to her mouth, muffling her scream of pleasure as she did exactly that.

His balls slammed her body as soon as he was in. The feeling was beyond mesmerizing. He slid out, shuddering with her, to the point where only the mushroom of his head was still encased in her. Then he plunged in again, gripped in the glove of her channel. His senses went to fire. His cock was searing steel, threatening to melt everything in its path. And she was telling him how *she* needed this?

"Christ." He growled it between thrusts. "You're so tight, so velvety." He grabbed both sides of her ass and positioned her for his deeper possession. "So *mine.*"

"Yes," she cried back. "Yes, Sir!"

"Say it." He drilled into her searing softness, pounding hard as he could. "Tell me who you belong to. Say it!"

"You." She was an image of pure submissive glory, her wrists coiling against the raffia, her thighs bunching, her neck strained. "You, Sir! I belong only to— Oh! Ohhhh!"

"One more second, honey." He controlled her completely now, using her body like a cylinder to his piston, pushing them both to the edge of combustion. "It'll be so good, I promise. Hold it back. One more second."

"I can't! I need to—"

"To what? Say it, Rose. What do you need?"

"Can't...speak. So hard to even think."

"Focus. Using your mind will help you restrain your pussy. What do you need?"

"Please, Sir. I need to come. I need to come!"

"Perfect."

He bit off his reply through clenched teeth, his eyes rolling back into his head from the effort. Her walls coiled around him like relentless bondage rope, yet he kept up the pace, knowing exactly where he'd rub her, inside and out. He loved what shock waves it'd set off in every precious inch of her pussy, hips, and thighs.

"Do it for me. Come hard around me, pet. *Now.*"

She keened and gasped, slamming her head back as every muscle in her body tensed. A scream erupted from her lips. Her tunnel convulsed around him. Mark groaned and gripped her, his hands brutal on her hips. The undulations of her orgasm twisted the come from him. The world became a billion fuses, his body a nuclear bomb of pleasure. Through every second of it, he focused on every sound, every tremor, and every breath she gave, joined to her, absorbed in her...

God help him, consumed by her.

How was this possible? How could she have been a stranger four days ago and now the person on earth to whom he felt most connected? It had only taken a spark or two, and now they were a forest fire, raging through the thick forests they'd both grown in their hearts.

But fire was fragile. Especially when half the kindling of one began to shudder, sob, and writhe against her restraints.

With quick tugs on the raffia, he unraveled the gauntlets

at her wrists. He gently lifted the tie off her eyes as well. As he expected, she reached and clung to his neck while he stroked the circulation back into her legs. He stayed inside her, taking their rhythm to slow strokes. "It's okay," he soothed. "Let it go. This is part of giving it to me too."

"Damn it," she muttered after several long minutes. "I'm sorry. I'm not always like this after sex."

"You're also not used to having sex like *this*."

"Do people really...get used to it?"

"Why would you want to?" He brushed her lips with his. "I hope I make you break down every time. I love your tears, honey. All of them. Your submission moves me."

He let his gaze roam her face. His words had drawn a definite question mark there. But he smiled, realizing he already knew what the question was. So they'd only known each other a little over a hundred hours. Big fucking deal. *He knew her.* And he saw she longed to believe it too—that she yearned to know a hundred hours was just the beginning of thousands, millions more.

"Yes," he told her, stroking both her temples. "I said every time. And I mean it. Listen...Rose...we'll talk about this. We'll figure it out."

A thunderous growl from her stomach eclipsed any answer she had for his declaration.

He laughed, and she matched it with a giggle. "What?" she quipped. "Somebody kept me from having dinner last night!"

Mark shot her his version of the evil eye. "I didn't hear any complaining."

"No, Sir. No complaining."

He reveled in her soft, content smile. For an instant, he caught something else on her features—something looking very much like...confidence. The stare of a woman who'd discovered something incredible in herself and not only recognized it but embraced it.

"I like this," he murmured with his own grin.

Her brows scrunched. "You like what?"

"Looking at you, without an inch of guilt or hesitation on your face." He kissed both her blushing cheeks before rolling off the bed and grabbing a pair of shorts from his suitcase. "Yet at the moment, I'm off to get something to satisfy that tiger in your stomach."

She laughed as he pulled on a formfitting black T-shirt. "Easy there, Tarzan. Chasing down a wildebeest won't be necessary. I just need some tea and fruit." She curled to her side, one thigh hooked atop the sheet, tempting him with her half-exposed backside. "Can't we just order something in?"

"Not a bad idea." He lowered his lips to her mouth again. "But I'm introducing you all to the Baghdad site leader via web conference today, and I want to be sure the equipment's ready to go. I'll swing by the kitchens on my way back. You like fruity teas, right? With some lemon?"

Her eyes widened. "You don't miss much."

"No." He got quiet with the reply. "I don't."

"Hmmm. Why do I think I should be worried?"

"Because you're dying to give me something to flog out of you?" As her mouth popped open, he snickered. "Okay, here's the agreement. No floggings today if there isn't any worrying today. You're forbidden to worry about anything for the next twenty-four hours. That includes all the self-doubts and all the internal backtalk. Got it?"

"Is that a direct order?"

"Yeah." He grabbed her hand, compelling her to look up

into his newly serious gaze. "It is."

She kissed his knuckles. "Very well, then. Anything else on that list, Sir?"

"Hmm." He trailed his hungry gaze over the curve of her thigh. "I can think of a few, but here's the first. Don't move. Be waiting for me, exactly like that, when I return."

She broke into a giggle. The sound was kittenish, sexy, and adorable. She compounded the effect by rolling over to expose one breast. "Yes, *Sir*!"

He chuckled and groaned, adjusting his hardness through his shorts. He remembered the first time she'd called him Sir and all the different ways he'd fantasized about hearing the word trip off her lips. This reality beat every one of those dreams.

This reality was so fucking *right.*

As he left the villa and headed for the resort's main building, the resolve grew stronger. It was the reason he'd decided to take the beach route. But the sand wasn't his destination because he wanted to hide his head in it. He needed to dig his feet into the earth as he delved his thoughts into the perplexity of Rose Fabian.

He couldn't delude himself about the bullet train upon which they'd jumped. He knew damn well this wasn't a conventional way to court a woman. Humans were complex creatures, with women the most dazzling examples. Knowing someone after four days was supposed to be impossible. But he'd also declared he'd never be this fulfilled again. Alone was something he'd gotten used to. Alone had always felt the better choice over the silly come-ons and flirtations on the Hill—even during the times it became loneliness.

Lonely was better than empty.

But Rose...

Filled the emptiness. Overflowed it. And damn it, he was good for her too.

He wasn't delusional. He knew they only had a basic foundation here. He knew the world, especially the media, would label him a sex-starved lecher, her a scheming status seeker, and the pair of them as fools who'd let island breezes and mai tais get the better of them.

More importantly, he knew Rose still didn't believe a Dominant/submissive relationship could be normal or right. Could she be blamed? On the sole occasion she'd opened up to someone about her "alternative" tastes, the bastard had turned tail and left her at the wedding altar for it.

But best as he could figure, that incident wasn't the first time Rose had been made to feel a fool for who she was. Her self-inflicted brain beatings were the result of being held up, time and time again, as the cautionary tale for a social elite who maintained their power on threads of disapproval, censorship, and a social code as obsolete as it was ludicrous. And the more he spoke to her, hearing how ingrained the shit was in her psyche, the more he guessed the ones feeding her this diet of degradation were people on an intimate basis with her emotional triggers.

Her family.

Much like the storm clouds still strung in the sky, a mixture of light and darkness wove through his thoughts. Yet just as the rising sun promised to burn them away, so did the next image filling his head. He saw Rose at the crest of her climax this morning, her gaze awash in tears of joy and completion.

It was so right. It was so significant.

A chuff slipped out. The irony of the impression didn't

escape him. He'd accomplished much as a senator, crafting laws to help millions of people and serving on committees that influenced millions more. All of it fell in the world's textbook definition of "significant."

All of it turned to dust when he thought of Rose after that orgasm.

Her beautiful face...

The face of a woman who'd discovered her power for the first time in her life.

In letting him have the control, and therefore all the worry, she'd given *herself* the freedom to explore her deepest passions, her wildest arousal. Her best and strongest self. In doing so, she'd become *his* revelation. His miracle. The key that had unlocked *his* power again. And if the world didn't understand that, it could kiss his rock-hard ass.

He broke into a jog as he headed toward the lobby. It was time to be in a hurry. His beautiful submissive was waiting for him.

CHAPTER TWELVE

Maybe, Rose thought, *I'm stuck in another reality.*

If so, she never wanted to leave.

She stretched and sighed between the sheets, giggling when realizing she'd just sniffed all the pillows simply because they still smelled like him: a little bit of wind, a little bit of spice, a hell of a lot of man. After finding the one with the strongest scent and going a little light-headed from inhaling too deeply, she tossed the thing to the side. The ceiling fan overhead turned lazily, making her dizzier. Or maybe that was the whirl of her thoughts.

"All right," she muttered. "Admit it. You're smitten."

She wanted to laugh at that too.

A ragged sigh escaped instead.

She was more than smitten.

Broadsided.

Swept away.

Terrified.

Yep. *Terrified for the win.*

She closed her eyes, focusing on the words—no, the promise—he'd given her just a few minutes ago.

We'll talk about this. We'll figure it out.

Warmth suffused her face. But most importantly, it filled her heart. And inside that heart, three soft words resounded.

I believe you.

Her breath hitched. She pressed fingers to her lips. Oh

God. *Did* she believe him? Could she really break herself open for a man again? Not just a few selections of herself either. Unlike Owen or anyone before him, Mark wanted everything. Could she turn over *all* of herself, *all* of the time, and expect to be accepted, treasured, safe?

The answer to that, in either direction, turned her into a frozen block.

The phone on the nightstand blared into her reverie.

She forced steadiness to her hands. "Stop it and chill. They're looking for Mark, not you."

Sure enough, after half a dozen rings, the caller hung up.

Thirty seconds later, the rings began again.

She used the bathroom, determinedly ignoring them.

On the third attempt, she glared at the contraption. "It's called a cell phone. It's in his pocket. You think of using *that* number?"

When round four began, she sighed—until thinking it might be Mark himself, calling and needing her for some reason. Or—shit—maybe it was an emergency from Washington or from GRI that couldn't be trusted to cell lines.

She dived for the receiver.

"Uhhh, good morning. Senator Moore's—"

What? Office? Villa? Den of decadent Dominance and submission?

Just like the white-hatted cowboy he evoked, Brandt Howell took over the line. "Mornin', Ms. Fabian. My sincere apologies for cuttin' in so soon after sunup, but the senator didn't want to be disturbed last night and gave me his cell to monitor for calls. About a half hour ago, damn thing started goin' off wilder than a fire alarm in a hay barn at a fireworks convention. Didn't recognize the number, so I disregarded it at first, but apparently the bastard got hold of it from someone high-up at GRI, and the shithead hasn't stopped since."

"What is it?" Her heart stopped, picking up his uncomfortable undertone. "The senator will be back in a minute, Brandt. Has something happ—"

"Actually, Ms. Fabian, the caller's looking for you."

"What?" Her pulse returned, but it sped with trepidation. "Me? But how does anybody know I'm...uh..." *Lying in the man's bed with scrapes on my arms from where he tied me up and then gave me the best orgasm of my life?*

"Hey, nobody else knows. Don't worry. I've got your back as well as the senator's. But this guy tried your cell a bunch of times and then got on the line to the hotel's security team, who were also instructed not to bother the senator. So they routed him to me, and here we are."

"Shane." The word spilled out as the gears of logic clicked together in her head.

"Who?"

"My brother," she explained. "The MO fits. He's a little persistent."

There was a commiserating snort from the line. "Maybe the senator should keep him in mind if he ever runs for office again."

"Right." She knew Brandt wouldn't mind her inability to muster a laugh. At the moment, possible reasons for Shane's urgency jabbed her mind like hornets, with the same reaction: a little irritation, a little fear. He was going through a lot of trouble to get to her, which meant he was wound up. And Shane never got wound up over *good* news.

"So you want them to patch the call through?"

"Yes, please." She forced a smile to the words. "Thanks, Brandt."

Through the next ten seconds, she pulled the covers tighter against herself and again reached for the pillow that smelled so much like Mark. She set her chin. Though there was no way for Shane to see, she hoped he'd hear it. No, she'd make him hear it. If she couldn't summon the strength for herself yet, she was going to be more clear, more determined, for Mark.

"Hello? Hello? Who the hell am I talking to *now?*"

She sighed. "Shane, calm down. It's me."

"Rose! Thank fucking God, at last!"

A giggle slipped out before she could stop it. "Wow. Congratulations, brother. You *do* know how to use the big-boy words."

"Don't start now, Rose. *Please* not now with the sarcastic sass. I've been trying to reach you for two hours on your cell. Where the hell are you?"

She swallowed and kept her chin up. "You know where I am. Apparently, you're on a first-name basis with every member of the resort's security team now too."

"Who all tell me you weren't answering the door at your room. So you know damn well what I'm really asking."

"Wait. You sent them to my—" She rolled her eyes. "Never mind. I should've known you'd do that." She took a steadying breath. "All right, so I'm not in my room. I'm a grown-up, Shane. And I'm not out in the middle of the beach with someone—"

"I should hope to hell not!" A scuffle filled the line. She practically saw him pacing his chic apartment overlooking the river, gazing out on the spectacular view but not even seeing it. "Sweet heaven, Rose, please tell me you're being discreet. If word got out you've been sleeping around at this 'training'—"

"What? *What*, Shane?"

Her spine went stiff, feeling like a lightning rod of

frustration was jammed up it. How many other times had she felt like this, charred yet soaked, absorbing the jolts of his and Mother's judgment? But that was her part to play, right? The one who always laughed too loud and smiled too wide, who felt too much and spoke too honestly. Because of it all, she'd cost the family an alliance that would have...

Gotten her a lifetime of the exact same thing.

Suddenly, she saw the universe's wisdom in absolutely everything that had happened to her.

Thank *God*.

"Spit it out, brother." Oddly, Shane's stunned silence made her smile. "Come on, tell me. Exactly what *would* happen if I indulged in some 'island delight' with one of my colleagues? Maybe more than one? Isn't that what everyone's talking about anyway? Isn't that what you and Mother have been busy with lately, more *Rose damage control*? How many committees did Mother have to sacrifice herself to in order to make everyone forget I'm actually off—gasp—helping the world?"

She braced herself for his signature huff or perhaps the sneering laugh Shane had perfected at one of the city's leading legal teams through the years. When he gave her only thick silence, she got a little scared.

"Mother hasn't had time for any more volunteer projects. She's been filing for bankruptcy."

She took her own turn for silence. Hers resonated with shock. "But how? Why?"

"Stay calm. I'm having enough trouble keeping Mother tethered." The huff finally came. "Thank God for sedatives."

"Sedatives?" She felt her lips pursing as she echoed the word, her concern real. What was Shane getting at, throwing in a word like that? Her brother had more fathoms than the

Mariana Trench, murkier now because of the real fear he'd stirred. Yes, Mother was childish and superficial, but she was still family. Their *mother*. "What are you saying? Is there an emergency? Is she all right?"

"She's fine, Rose. Did I say she wasn't?"

Aside from just implying their mother was sucking down her martinis in pill form every four hours, she supposed he hadn't. "I really don't understand," she stated. "Father left her millions in the settlement. Even so, if she sold off just half her furs and jewelry, she'd regain a nice part of it."

"Not going to happen." There was a decisive pause, as if Shane was squaring up his stance. "She's going to need them. We're moving forward with a new plan."

She stifled the urge to let out another laugh, this one not so amused. "Of course we are. Which is why you're calling." The impetus for his urgency in reaching her began to crystallize. He wanted to make sure he still had the marionette strings attached to her, the control still wielded.

She shook her head. Control. What a chameleon of a word. She'd hated it all her life, equating it to sleepless nights of pondering Shane's catalogs of her mistakes at some dinner or agonizing over what shoe Mother would approve of for the charity tea or, in true Eliza Doolittle fashion, wondering what *was* appropriate to yell at one's horse at the racetrack. In her world, control was about containment, reins, and everything she couldn't be. But Mark had changed that. In his hands, the term had become a gift, a treasure she gladly gave because of the world he opened in return, tying her in a connection she'd craved forever. Something so different than the irritation now jabbing her, courtesy of the voice on the other end of the line.

"Every minute right now counts, Rose." Shane's tone

gained a new edge. "Every move we make, all three of us, will count from here. So, yes, that's why I'm calling."

She pulled in a deep breath, desperately wishing Mark had returned by now. She imagined him next to her, tawny eyes glittering, a half smile jerking at his lips. "All right. Let's have it, then. What's this spectacular new plan?"

She could almost smell her brother's anticipation through the line. "Do you remember Tristan Rouselle?"

"Yes." She said it as if telling a four-year-old the earth was really round. "It's hard to forget one of the founders of your God's-gift-to-the law firm, Shane."

Instead of the defensive snort for which she braced, her brother actually laughed. "He's on the governor's short list to fill Mark Moore's seat in the senate. It was announced yesterday morning."

Her stomach tightened. So it *was* the last thing she expected to hear. But the announcement tripped her less than the tie-in to Mark. Even hearing his name on Shane's lips... It bridged her old caterpillar to her new butterfly like a tenacious cocoon that wouldn't fall free.

"Okay." She used sarcasm to mask her anxiety. "And?"

"And we're going to help him land it."

"Now I'm lost. Help him? He can't run for a seat in Indiana, can he? And if so, how's he going to do it with Mother's furs and jewels?"

"Rose." Now it seemed like *she* was the four-year-old. "He's got a bigger house in Indianapolis than he does in Chicago. And he's single."

"Yes. So is Mark Moore." Her guts took her by surprise again. They definitely didn't like the sound of that.

"But he wasn't when he got elected. A successful candidate needs a good woman."

Understanding glimmered. "And Mother is going to be that woman for Tristan."

"You mean Senator Rouselle?" He chuckled again, jerking them forward by a few years. Now they were eleven, and he was beating the pants off her at backgammon—only the playing pieces were people, and the stakes were no longer piles of M&Ms.

"And what if 'Senator Rouselle' doesn't see her as that woman?"

"That won't be an option."

She wanted to roll her eyes, but Shane had ridiculed that out of her years ago. Even in a phone conversation, she didn't dare. "And that's where the plan comes in."

She listened to him take a hefty swig of a drink. Since it was six thirty a.m. in Chicago, it was likely his daily cup of custom-blended coffee. "The public devours good love stories, sister. They crave a gooey fairy tale. But with most political candidates, they have to hear about it after the fact. Tristan and Mother are going to let them live the story as it happens. She's going to become their real-life princess."

"And as her prince, Tristan rides to the senate."

"And maybe, in a few years...beyond."

Shane's endgame turned glaringly clear. He'd probably scoped out the floor plan of the White House and already picked out his office. Scary truth was, it wasn't an unrealistic hope. She remembered rumors of the same thing swirling about Mark himself last summer.

But all of it still confused her in one distinct, disconcerting way.

"Shane, I'm still not sure why you plowed your way through half the phone lines and most of the security team in

ANGEL PAYNE

this place to tell me this." She picked a nervous finger at the corner of the bed sheet. "It's not like I'm going to be around to screw things up for you, right?" She held out a tiny hope, fizzling fast, that *this* time he'd deny the implication—that he'd protest how proud he really was of her for doing this. And Lake Michigan would sprout real icebergs. "In two weeks, I'll be almost ten thousand miles away."

"And Mark Moore is training you to get there, right?"

Her stomach clenched tighter. "Yes. What does he have to do with—"

"He's your teacher, right? And nothing more?"

She swung a wild stare around the room. Shane's tone... It made her search for hidden cameras they didn't know about. Or maybe his question would morph into a laser beam, slicing across the miles and exposing her here, clad in nothing but the sheets Mark had ripped from her body...

"Wh-What the hell kind of question is that?"

"Listen, Rose. Tying yourself to the headboard for Owen was a tough enough mess to clean up, but this is a new playing field. It's muddy, it's brutal, and it's not for a little green nymph to run around in with her knickers at her knees. You'll get hurt—and this pain will be deep wounds, not knee scrapes. The collateral damage will be insurmountable. The press has already started sniffing around at the firm. Not the glossy tabloids either. This is the *Times*, the nightly news stations, CNN..."

As he droned on, she clawed her hair with a shaking hand. *A messy playing field.* She already felt dragged through the mud, though Shane technically hadn't gotten the details right. She hadn't really tied herself to the headboard that fateful night at the Fairmont. She'd never gotten that far.

The memories hit, so clear now, of how dashing Owen had looked when they'd gotten back to their suite after the rehearsal dinner. He'd had a Scotch or two more than his norm, making him pretty frisky, especially because she'd put up a playful protest about not "doing the deed" so close to the wedding. She'd looked at his growing erection and his heavy gaze and decided to get bold. *"Have I been a bad girl, my love? Do you need to spank me? Do you need to do it hard?"*

He'd bolted from the room thirty seconds later.

She'd never seen him again.

Her face burned with the humiliation again, though time had dulled its impact a little. There was also another strange difference to the memory. She'd always remembered the look on Owen's face from that moment and assumed it was revulsion. Now, she recognized it for its truth.

Fear.

There were a lot of words she could use to describe Mark Moore. *Fearful* was nowhere in the neighborhood of that list.

Then why did her heart pummel at her ribs with a deafening cadence?

Why was this entire conversation making her body taut, her head throb, and her heart hurt?

For an answer, she only had to think of the fact that Shane had called, period. Her brother had hunted her down across the miles to remind her of one important fact. To him, to most of the world, she was still—how did it go?—*a little green nymph with her knickers around her knees.*

God.

If he only knew her "knickers" were already a soaked blob at the bottom of the pool.

Forget it. The point was made. Nothing had changed, had

it? She was still hardwired with the fuck-up chip, programming that didn't magically get erased by the submissive chip. She'd fail Mark, just as she'd failed Owen. But this time, as Shane had said so damn eloquently, the playing field was muddier.

And this time, she truly cared about the guy holding the ball. *Cared?* Oh God. She wished she was only at cared with Mark. With cared, the twist in her stomach wouldn't feel like a drain snake dipped in acid. With cared, she wouldn't be covering the sob in her mouth and the curse she longed to let fly at her brother. Why the hell had he waited to make this call? Had they done this yesterday morning, she'd never have caved to Mark's invitation or come to the villa. She never would've known the ecstasy of letting him turn her body into a thousand electric raindrops, her soul into a bird that gathered those drops and flew to the moon and back with them.

She never would've known the misery of now.

She slammed her forehead to her knees. Her gulps lodged like boulders in her throat.

"Rose? Rose, are you still there?"

"Y-Yeah. S-Sorry."

"So we have nothing to worry about, right?"

Shit, shit, shit.

"N-No, Shane. It's cool. Everything's good here."

"Perfect. Enjoy paradise, then."

As he hung up, she almost laughed. Paradise. Sure, if that's what you called this. What the hell *was* this? She'd never felt anything like it before. She'd been dying to get off the call so she could release the pressure in her chest, the agony in her body. But now, while everything ached behind her ribs, nothing broke free. Her eyes stung and her head throbbed, but the cries jammed at the base of her throat. Her bones were as stiff as wood. Her lips were as dry as sawdust.

Somehow she got herself off the bed and back into her half-soggy clothes. Falling into the chair at the desk in the next room, she focused on wrapping her fingers around the pen in the holder there and pressing letters into the resort stationery. Five minutes later, most of the pad was in the wastebasket, filled with her ridiculous attempts at putting this into words.

Everything was so lovely. Thank you for—
I had a wonderful time. But now—
It's not going to work out. I think we both know it. I'm not
that good at all this, and—
It's come to my attention that we'd best just—
I want you to know I'll never forget—
Senator Moore, thank you for a most enjoyable—

"Crap!"

The single word pulled free the cork on her dam of emotion. As the sobs finally came and her anguish flowed, she scribbled the only message that made complete sense.

I'm sorry.

CHAPTER THIRTEEN

Mark looked down at the paper in his hand and its two scribbled words and forced himself not to crunch it into a ball and hurl it across the training classroom. The wad was already half-destroyed from the first three times he'd done that. But continuing to vent his fury wouldn't get him anywhere right now. It wouldn't gain him any more clarity for the confusion that had hit when he arrived back at the villa, bearing a breakfast feast and a continuing hard-on, to find the bed empty, the trash can full, and the damn note on the table.

He'd instantly tried her cell—and gotten the voice mail he expected. He'd set the line to redial and let it do that a dozen times as he dumped the trash can and sifted through her first drafts of the note. They were novels by comparison to what she did leave but no more helpful to his anger, his bewilderment, and his determination to find out just what the *hell* had happened between her whispered "Yes, Sir" and her tear-stained "I'm sorry."

The trainees starting filing into the room. Brandt Howell was with them, determinedly picking his way through the crowd. The young man approached with his square jaw taut but his light-blue eyes glittering in victory.

"Senator Moore, sir."

Mark modulated his voice to a careful murmur. "Tell me you have good news, Brandt."

"You bet your sweet a— Yes, uhhh, I mean I do." The

security expert flashed an easygoing smile at a perky blonde who walked by as he unlocked his phone and showed the screen to Mark. "Since the call to Miss Fabian was routed through me, it was pretty easy to douse a few firewalls and trace the call. It's the private line of Shane Fabian, out of Chicago, exactly who she told me it would be. Her brother."

He nodded and handed the phone back to Brandt. "Okay. And what do we know about him?"

"He's a senior partner at Rouselle, Wright, and Treforth. Purchased a place overlooking the river about six months ago. Likes the swag and the designers, was seen in the social column a lot until the whole bang-bang-pow of Rose's wedding day. He's been starting to get back into the swing of things, though—working the connections..."

Mark held up his hand, fixing his thoughts to something in Brandt's account. "Rouselle, Wright, and Treforth. That's *Tristan* Rouselle's firm, right?"

"I believe so, sir."

"Thank you, Brandt. Really good work." He nodded at the phone. "Now erase all that."

Brandt punched a couple of keys, and the screen went black. "Done, sir."

Mark gave a deferential nod, universal guy code for his gratitude. He worked a finger over his bottom lip, weaving this new piece of information into the tapestry he already knew of his subbie's psyche. Despite the circumstances, it was a heartening thread to receive. She hadn't just bolted from the villa of her own accord as he'd originally assumed—and feared. There had been a phone call. Something had pulled at her tapestry all the way from the States and started unraveling it.

Okay, maybe the bastard had gotten beyond *started*. Mark

had only been gone from the villa for a half hour, tops. He'd left behind a woman with his beard burn on her cheeks, adoration in her eyes, and a confident smile on her lips. He'd come back to find that note on the table, dunked in a puddle of her tears. Whoever did that to her had done it before. Skillfully. Ruthlessly. Now he had a name for the asshole. And possibly, based on the details Brandt had just supplied, a workable reason for the call too. Not a pretty one, but right now, the only pretty thing he saw about Shane Fabian was the man's goddamn Gucci-ad hair.

He looked at Brandt again. "How are the other arrangements going?" he asked. "The special accommodations I requested for tonight? Any trouble?"

The Texan slid him another grin. "Not one, Senator. Everything'll be ready to roll by six."

"Perfect. Thank you, Brandt."

"My pleasure, Sena—holy *shit*!"

For the first time in the five days he'd known the man, Brandt Howell's veneer dissolved like the stick of butter it always seemed to be coated in. Mark watched in bemusement as the man's jaw popped and eyes bugged. A palpable frisson hit everyone else in the room too. Since the building was still standing, Mark ruled out a sudden hurricane.

Turned out it was a bigger force of nature.

His daughter.

Dasha fulfilled her pop goddess image in a sparkly T-shirt, formfitting jeans, and stilt heels that aged him by another year just by looking at them. Nothing like ensuring she'd get a ferocious hug, which he gave as soon as she raced close enough.

"Hi, Daddy!"

"Well hello there, beautiful."

"I wanted to surprise you!"

"You succeeded."

After releasing her, he shook hands with the two men who never seemed to leave her side these days. Her manager, David Pennington, and her security lead, Kress Moridian, both gave him respectful greetings and solid handshakes. Dasha kissed his cheek again, still completely unaware of Brandt standing there in speechless puppy love.

Mark joined a chuckle to her infectious laugh, letting her effervescence ease away the ache in his chest for a few moments. The love she always brought up in him, an eternal well of fierce emotion, was interrupted only when humor tapped. It was damn near impossible to ignore the way Moridian *and* Pennington turned into snarling gargoyles at poor Brandt, who now dared to inch forward, beholding Dasha like she was made of crystal.

Mark ignored all three of them, keeping his arms around Dasha in a proclamation to them all of who the *first* man was in her life. "Don't tell me you were just in the neighborhood?" he quipped.

Dasha giggled. "Sort of. Remember the concert dates I had to cancel last year in Miami?"

Mark nodded. Of course he remembered. The performances were postponed because of a phony stalker attempt staged by *his* whack job of a chief aide, who then decided to make them not so fake after all. The incident was one of the biggest reasons he'd said goodbye to active politics.

"We finally had a chance to reschedule the shows," Dasha went on. "Then added on a couple more. It was fun, but I'm wiped. We cleared a little break time, and I remembered you mentioning this training here, so...ta-da! I hope you don't mind?"

"*I* don't mind."

The quiet interjection came from Brandt, who'd turned a shade of crimson deserving its own crayon name. Dasha laughed again, taking Mark back to when she first learned to do that, getting him to buy her candy and hair bows at the Base Exchange.

"Hi," she said, extending her hand. "I'm Dasha."

"I know."

"So are you helping my dad stay in line?"

Brandt grinned slowly. "Miss Moore, I don't believe in lines."

"All right, cowboy." Mark stepped in as he noticed the I'm-gonna-tear-his-head-off look darkening Pennington's features. *And* Moridian's. He refused to look at, or translate, either of them any further. Some things were best for a father not to know, especially if his daughter looked deliriously happy about it. "Before everyone starts pissing in each other's cereal, you're all dismissed. I have business to conduct here."

"Excellent point." David stepped forward, managing to look all business despite ditching his beloved business threads for an open-necked shirt and jeans. "I'm sure they have our villa ready for us by now." He tugged at Dasha's waist, but she turned to Mark one last time.

"I think I'm going to get some sleep tonight, Daddy. Want to grab breakfast in the morning? Er...Dad? Dad?"

"Yes. Sure, darling."

He remembered getting the words out. Sort of. They left him just as the awareness of Rose took over again, picking up first on that subtle scent in the air, the smell locked into his soul by now. He braced himself for her beauty as the aroma wrapped around his senses, compelling his gaze toward her—

As she slid into a desk at the back of the room.

"Daddy? Are you okay?"

It took a conscious lock of every muscle in his body, backed by the reminder that forty more people now occupied the room, not to hurl furniture aside and fly to her.

"Fine, darling. See you soon."

No, damn it. I'm far from fine. Oh Rose...my pet...what the hell did that bastard say to you?

He forced himself to take it all in. Every painful inch. She'd scraped her hair back into a severe braid. Her eyes were swollen and bloodshot. Her forehead was crumpled as if she were lost, yet she curled a pashmina around her shoulders as if she never wanted to be found. He was a little relieved when a few of the other women noticed her and checked on her, concern on their faces. She gave them all brave smiles, likely making up some excuse about catching a flu bug of some sort and she'd be "back to her old self" by tomorrow.

He drew in a measured breath. Her old self? Not if he had anything to do with it.

A touch of doubt had lingered in his mind after he set the plans in motion for tonight, asking for Brandt's help with the logistical details. Now, staring again at his submissive in all her torn-down misery, he knew no other path was an option for her. For *them*.

Bolstered by that ultimatum, he hardened his stare. "Let's settle down and get started for the day, people. Open your study manuals to chapter fifteen. We're going to focus on your role not only as project leaders but project participants." He directed his eyes right at Rose as he finished. "Specifically, about knowing when you're supposed to listen to directions and follow orders."

He wasn't surprised when all he saw for the rest of the morning was the top of her head.

He also wasn't surprised when they returned from the lunch break and Veronica Vernon, clad in her typical New Orleans sparkles, approached him. "Senator Moore? Rose Fabian sends her regrets. She's not feeling well and went to her room. She wants you to know she'll be better by Monday."

"Thank you, Veronica." He smiled in return. "Tell her I relay wishes for a speedy recovery."

The young woman blinked thick black lashes. "Oh, I don't think I'll be seeing her, Senator. She says she's putting everything on do not disturb, and she plans on sleeping the weekend away."

"Perhaps that's for the best."

As Veronica took her seat, he looked up at the space Rose had occupied this morning, still remembering her devastated, slumped form. After tonight, she would never look that way again. He vowed it with every Dominant bone in his body, with every protective drop of blood in his veins.

"Go ahead and run, Rose—but you can't hide." Though he issued the pledge beneath his breath, it was wound with the steel of his resolve. "I'm coming for you, and we're going to fix it. We're going to do it together." He curved up one side of his mouth as he finished that dark, determined promise. "Rest for now. You're going to need it."

CHAPTER FOURTEEN

It would get better. She needed to just get through the next minute; then it would get better.

Another minute passed.

Why wasn't it getting better?

Rose lay on the floor in the middle of her room, stomach down. The carpet, rough against her swollen cheek, had become a strange friend. She focused on the abrasion of the fibers, using the little scrape of pain to pull her through to her next breath and then her next.

It would get better. She had to believe it. She was doing everything right so far. Seclusion. Bath. More seclusion. Quart of ice cream. Nap. Okay...attempt at nap. More seclusion. Lying on the floor. Crying into the carpet.

Damn it, it *had* to get better.

The rub was, she'd done this before. More than anyone on the planet, she knew the drill about making a mistake and then dealing with the self-hatred shit storm from it. This time she was even prepared. This time she'd declared herself the disaster before Mark could. Didn't the universe give credit for that? Didn't the agony dagger cut you a break for saving someone from yourself when *you* made the decision? Wasn't there a cauterization option for taking the high road into heartbreak, making it fast and easy, leaving behind relief of the emptiness?

A choked laugh left her. She knew about emptiness too.

That was the next joke. Empty wasn't relief. Empty was... empty. It was black-and-white, stripped of color. Stripped of Mark. And damn it, it was better this way. It had to be. He'd see that too. He was a brilliant man.

Oh God, so brilliant.

She'd miss him. His laughing insights about so many things. His stories about the Iraqi kids and their simple jokes. His magical descriptions of desert sunsets. His mouth-watering accounts about how good goat cheese and dates tasted on a piece of *samoon*.

"Shit."

Emptiness was hell.

She pushed to her knees, shoving back the hair chunks stuck to her soaked cheeks. A glance at the clock showed she was only a few hours into this ordeal. It felt like weeks. And she couldn't breathe. Even that felt like a function she had to think about, to wonder if she was doing the right way.

She jammed her room key into a pocket and wrenched the door open. The afternoon's session wasn't due to end for forty-five more minutes, so she had some time before having to dive into her cave again. The day was coming to an idyllic end, a wash of peach drenching the sky in preparation for a brilliant sunset. She sat on the low stone wall in front of her room and watched some people running along on the sand. A woman and two men laughed, chased, and yelled at each other. Rose envied their carefree peace. Envied it, even though she didn't understand it. That sort of happiness...well, she just wasn't destined for it.

Didn't deserve it.

She was so absorbed in watching the laughter on the trio's faces, she didn't realize they were tossing something around.

A soft basketball emblazoned with the Bulls logo. She knew that part of it now because the ball suddenly bonked her on the head.

"Oh my gosh." The woman, a stunning blonde, ran over. "We are so, so sorry!"

"It's his fault," shouted one of the men, a cutie in a Miami Dolphins T-shirt.

"Suck my banana, fruit face," the second retorted.

"Sirs?" the woman called back. "A dull roar on that, please?" She flashed a grin belonging on a movie star at Rose. "I'm really sorry. They're usually very nice, when they haven't spent the majority of the morning cooped up on a plane."

Rose extended the ball back to her with a forced smile—which suddenly dropped. "You're Dasha Moore."

The pop star's face softened with recognition too. "And you're the one who made my dad turn to mush this morning."

Grief stabbed all over again. She turned away. "I'm sorry. I didn't mean to." *I never meant to hurt him. I just want him to be happy.*

"Bummer," Dasha muttered. "Because my dad hasn't been mushy in a really long time." She chuckled. "Did you know I tried fixing him up with Gwen Stefani, pre-Blake? Even she wasn't mush-worthy. My dad's a damn finicky mush-giver."

"He's a good person." She looked Dasha in the eyes as she stated it. It succeeded in relaying her sincerity but invited in a fresh wave of heartache. The woman shared her father's gaze, down to the yes-I'm-reading-your-mind intensity.

After a contemplative moment, Dasha sat on the wall too. "So what's your name?"

"Rose. Well, Rosalind. I'm in your dad's class. I guess you figured that out." Funny. She hadn't been nervous with the gorgeous pop star until now. She wished they could just talk about Gwen Stefani again. "He's a good teacher. A good man. A really good man. He deserves..."

Everything. So much more than me.

"D!" The man with the tousled dark hair and the lean build shouted up the sand. "Come on, sweetheart!"

"Or do we need to...come for you?" yelled the other.

Rose couldn't help joining her giggle to Dasha's. The woman swept her luxurious gold mane from her eyes and smiled back at them. "Two more secs? Please?" She hurled the ball back, and they both dived for it, wrestling in a tangle of limbs and grunts. "There," she muttered. "That ought to keep the puppies occupied for a bit."

Despite her teasing tone, Dasha gazed at the men like they were a pair of half-god gladiators. Rose couldn't help but stare at the open adoration on her face. When the young woman caught her gaping and laughed again, Rose stuttered, "S-Sorry. Why don't you go back to your...uh...friends. I was just—"

"Trying to figure out a little mush of your own?"

She took in a sharp breath and bowed her head. Crap, what else would Dasha see on her features?

Seemed the woman inherited her father's stubbornness too.

"Rose." She closed their fingers together. "It's not my place to pry, but I can tell you this. I almost let doubt and fear rope me back from having the greatest joy of my life. It took me nearly getting killed to realize it." She coiled her grip tighter, compelling Rose to look at her again. "I'm serious. It took a gun barrel at my forehead for me to get the point."

Dasha tilted her face out toward the water, where a number of boats floated by on the sparkling azure expanse.

"Life doesn't give you a lot of chances to grab happiness, you know? When the anchor's pulled up, then you'd better sail that ship for everything you're worth."

She drew in another deep breath. She knew Dasha meant every word, and she yearned to absorb it all into her heart and make it her truth too—but one unalterable truth would never make it her own reality. As that truth roped its way around her heart again, she pulled free from Dasha and stood.

"Not if you're the one who can't read the map, Dasha. Not if you're the one who's going to run the ship into the rocks and kill everyone."

★ ★ ★

Deeming the fresh-air quest a fail, she rushed back to her room and wept through another long bath. Then another attempt at a nap.

TV, maybe?

Sure, that turned out to be *real* productive. After clicking past three horrible reality shows, two bad sitcom reruns, and another showing of *Titanic*, she plunged the room into silence again.

And once more decided to curl up on the floor.

"You have to stop this."

She snarled it at herself, watching her fingers clutch the carpet.

"Damn it." She forced her hand into a fist. "You need to deal with this, Ro. You *are* going to deal with this. You had a life without him before. Okay, so it was half a life by comparison, but at least it was..."

Who the hell was she kidding?

She didn't have a map for this.

The best thing to do was squeeze her eyes shut, let the pain come, and attempt to hang on.

"One minute at a time," she whispered. "One minute at a—"

A pounding at the door sliced into her mantra.

She gritted her teeth. The housekeepers on shift today apparently didn't know how to read their own Do Not Disturb signs. This was the fourth time one of them had tried to get in. This one was persistent. She forced herself to sit up, but she didn't move from the floor. As the urgent knocks continued, she ran Vegas-style bets in her head about the odds of a sweet little maid being mighty enough to break in a solid wood door in the name of fresh towel delivery.

"Rosalind Fabian!"

The booming voice stopped her heart.

"Shit!" It was barely a breath on her lips.

"Rose, I won't knock again. Open the damn door!"

She stumbled to her feet. But then froze. Raw energy spiked her bloodstream, followed by a sluice of fear. Mark's bellow was a battering ram of fury. She stumbled back, shaking her head in quick little jerks. "I...I can't. Please, go away! Go away and try to understand!"

"Rose!"

She retreated as far from the door as she could, palming the tears from her face and falling into a chair next to the patio slider. "I won't do this. I can't do this. I break everything I touch, and damn it, I won't break you! Just forget me and— *Shit!"*

The oath spilled out of her on half a scream. She got the sound out as a figure in black cargo pants, black T-shirt, and a matching thunderhead of a glower hoisted over the fence onto her patio. She was amazed Mark's beard hadn't gone the shade of ink too, as he slammed the slider back and stomped into the room.

His presence threatened to stretch the walls. His stare was filled with fire. She curled in on herself, despite every cell of her body thrumming back to life, as he approached and then braced in front of her chair. He literally loomed over her.

"I told you I wouldn't knock again."

She jerked her chin up, reacting to his King-of-Siam tone, but almost lowered it again. That was when she saw what her attitude did to him. Even through his rage, his mouth parted, his gaze narrowed, and the juncture of his thighs swelled. He really wasn't afraid of her. He *wanted* her strength.

But this wasn't about what he wanted. Or what she did either. Sometimes life wasn't about a kiss from kismet and a happy ending. She'd walked in his stratosphere for a few incredible hours. It had to be enough. Anything more, and she was bound to misstep so badly, she'd tumble out of his cloud—and bring the whole thing down with her too. Then she'd stumble from the mess she'd made, only to watch him bolt out the door, carrying half her heart with him.

Half? Who was she kidding? He already had that much.

"Look, if you want an explanation, I'll do my best to—"

"Stand up."

His tone didn't brook a shred of rebellion. Rose complied and then instantly balked. Where the hell was this going to get them?

"Fine." She jerked up her jaw. "You want to talk. I get that. So let's sit down like adults, and—"

"Where's your phone and your purse?"

She blinked. "Pardon me?"

But by then, he'd spotted her cell and her purse. He stomped over, scooped them up, and then tossed the first into the second. "You can bring these," he stated. "And that's it."

"Bring them—"

"Let's go."

"What the—*no*!"

When he only responded by stomping across the room and jerking the door open, letting in the peach-and-orange light of the coming sunset, she locked her hands to her hips.

"*Mark*. Damn it. What the hell is—*ahhhh*!"

She screamed as the world tipped over—and she realized the man had swung her up and over his shoulder. With the world flipped and his biceps wrapped around her middle, she barely had a chance to comprehend he'd carried her right out the door.

"Are you freaking kidding me? *Seriously*, Pirate Pete?"

He didn't say a word. Just skirted the beach, now arriving at the resort's dock.

"Are you really doing this? Because carrying me off on your galleon will *not* extract a damn confession."

"It's not your time to talk, Rose." His steps were determined and steady on the heavy planks of the dock. "There's going to be plenty of time for that. But not now."

He approached an expansive sailboat she didn't remember seeing at the dock this week. Though the ship's hull was cut in a modern design, everything from the deck up was really and truly an ode to pirate decadence, with rigging, yardarms, and two sails ready to be hoisted. If she were in a more dignified position, she would've stopped to admire the polished wood, gleaming fixtures, and obvious care given to the boat—but right now, maintaining equilibrium was a bigger priority.

The task got more complicated when he flipped her back over and set her to her feet. He kept one hand locked on her wrist as she tried to gain back some dignity along with her balance.

"You okay?" The words were sincere though his tone was tight.

"Reasonably."

"Good. Then we'll start things here."

"Things? Wh-What do you mean, things?"

He answered as if she hadn't spoken. "You know your safe word. Use it if you need to." He grabbed her chin, forcing her face up. "Using your safe word to avoid a question does *not* qualify as need." With another sweep of command, he stepped back and used a jerk of his head to back up his order. "Now get on board."

His voice, so full of that no-isn't-an-option timbre, still made her hesitate. It had nothing to do with fearing for her physical safety. She knew, deep into her gut, Mark would never lead her into danger.

Her decision dealt with a bigger peril. If she got on the boat, he expected her to talk. To tell him everything. To completely bare her heart and soul to him.

It was going to be hard.

She didn't want to do this.

She wanted to do this more than anything.

She couldn't just sail off into the sunset with him.

Could she?

Rose looked up into the ropes, rigging, and sails of the magnificent vessel. And like the breeze gently swaying them, words filled her mind as if brought by the cosmos themselves.

Life doesn't give you a lot of chances to grab happiness,

Rose. When the anchor's pulled up, then you'd better sail that ship for everything you're worth.

She bowed her head.

And walked down the gangway.

She knew damn well how selfish the choice was. This wasn't going to be easy, nor was it going to be forever—but for a little while more, Mark would be her captain. Her Dom. Completely *hers*.

She latched on to the feeling, relishing how her heart soared, her blood raced...and her pussy clenched. Maybe he knew that already—though she doubted it changed his plan. He'd clearly thought this through. She contemplated that in full, looking around as he helped the skipper release the ropes off the vessel. Precision planning like this was usually inspired by one of two things. Rage or lust.

How much trouble was she in if his incentive had been both?

He walked toward her as they motored toward the horizon. She'd been trying to appreciate the cottony cirrus feathers floating across the sunset sky, but they were overshadowed by the black clouds in his gaze. He kept his distance from her with a wide, braced posture, as if trying to chisel his way into her brain from the outside in, making her shift on her feet with more discomfort by the minute.

Finally, she couldn't take the standoff anymore. "Did you do all this just to stand there and glare at me?"

"I'm asking the questions right now, Rose. And I expect answers. Honest ones."

She wet her lips. "Fine. Ask away. You'll get them."

"Will I?" His words seared like blowtorches. "How do I know that?" At her questioning stare, he turned up the flames even hotter. "I thought I was getting honesty from you this morning. I thought you really meant those *Yes, Sirs*. I thought you liked being there, in my bed, waiting for me."

"I did." She stepped to him, trying to grab his arm. "I meant it! Every word!"

"Bullshit." The wind whipped at his hair, making his snarling features an even more daunting sight. "You left! And this—" He yanked out her note from this morning, now creased in a million places. "*This* doesn't constitute asking permission to leave!"

She endured a war of emotions. Part of her ached to take the paper back, tear it to pieces, and then toss it to the wind. Did he think it had been easy to write that? Even if it had, his permission wasn't required, damn it! The last time she checked, the Victorians and their restrictions had been evicted from the Bahamas.

But another part of her, the part that had broken free for him, *because* of him this week, acknowledged his words.

Then embraced them.

And yes, needed them.

Even the fury in them.

He had his own easier choices than this...than her. *A lot* of them. Apparently, even dates with Gwen Stefani. But here he was, on a boat he'd gotten from God-knew-where, after he'd literally pulled her off her feet and carried her here, fighting for her with every ounce of his being.

And just like that, a little more of her heart slipped away in his grasp.

Tears. She tried to force them back but ended up choking. "I...I'm sorry. You deserve an explanation. I...I'll try to give it to you now."

He jammed the note back into his pocket. "And I'll believe you why?"

She spread her hands. "I haven't openly lied to you."

He grabbed her wrists and shoved them down. "The fuck you haven't." Surging close, aligning his face inches from hers, he glared with eyes like stoked coals. "You agreed to an instruction of your Sir, and then you defied it. So yes, you essentially lied, Rose."

"I didn't defy you!" She pushed back again, but there wasn't anywhere to go. He was close enough to pin her in now, and he did, blocking out the sky with his damnable, beautiful nearness. "I mean, it wasn't my intention!" She couldn't help it anymore. The tears broke free. "And I can't ever call you Sir again, so it doesn't matter anyway. It was a ridiculous dream, Senator—and now it's over."

CHAPTER FIFTEEN

Mark's breath left him in an agonizing rush.

Senator.

He'd expected her apology. He'd even expected her to protest about her disobedience being unintentional, that it had been because of things beyond her control. Then he'd expected her to accept his forgiveness for the former, his swift punishment for the latter, and then his direct order, as her Dominant, to tell him exactly what the fuck had happened in that half hour he'd been gone. Then together they'd deal with her asshole of a brother and move on.

It wasn't going to be that easy.

Senator.

It wasn't just the goddamn word itself. It was how she'd said it. Defeat underlined every note. The finishing dip of her head could've placed her at a funeral.

She'd really given up. Not just on them and on him, but worse, on herself, on that piece of her soul that had finally pushed free and lived at the villa last night. Her spiritual release had been as beautiful to behold as her physical climaxes.

That bastard brother of hers had shoved all of it right back into a cage.

But so help him God, they weren't getting off this boat until he found the key again.

He watched Rose grow restless beneath his scrutiny. She only wore a T-shirt and shorts, and the setting sun illuminated her pebbled nipples, her wriggling hips. Good. This was good. Her words denied him, but her body sure as fuck didn't.

He pressed a little closer. Sure enough, the heat from her skin ticked higher. "A dream," he murmured. "And you've woken up, is that it?"

Oddly, she looked relieved he'd said that. "Right. Yes."

He contemplated her reaction. She was still on edge, but he could tell she hedged an inner hunch, maybe thinking he'd gotten fed up enough to let things lie here. And why not? It was the shit she'd gotten from every other significant man in her life. A completely absent father. A fiancé who'd walked out on her wedding day. Coworkers, threatened by her strength, who teased. And a brother who used all of it to make her fit his own cookie-cutter brand of behavior. She clearly thought he was like all of them. She was clearly wrong.

But right now, she didn't know that. And she wouldn't believe it either, even if he climbed to the top of the mast and declared it to the whole ocean. Why would she?

He had to show her. And he would have to get sneaky about it.

"Okay," he said. "If that's how you're going to spin it, then that's how we'll roll."

"R-Really?"

"Yep." He pushed back but resumed his resolute stance. "If that's how you feel after your punishment, then that's what I'll honor. You have my word as a man and a Dom."

Her follow-up to that was also what he expected. A bunch more blinks. A puzzled frown. "Wait. After my *what?*"

He prefaced his comeback by stripping off his shirt. The move was completely calculated. He knew how formidable he looked now, standing there with his chest bare, his hands clasped at his back, the wind shoving his hair, his gaze a direct drill into hers. "You heard me, Rose. You want to be free from me, from our dynamic, then fine—but you'll fulfill your obligation to it first. You say you left this morning for reasons beyond your control. I believe you. But since you've chosen not to share the reasons with me, I have no choice but to punish you for the defiance."

Her mouth popped open. But her breasts jutted hard against her clothes, their defined buds proving how his tone affected her. "You're not kidding, are you?"

He dropped his scrutiny to the juncture of her thighs. She'd crossed her legs. *Very* tight. "Do you want to test me and find out?"

She tried to laugh. The effort was feeble. And adorable. "And what if I refuse?"

He shrugged, another intended move. "You have that prerogative." He raised his arm, pressing his elbow to the bulkhead next to her head. "But I don't think you want to exercise it." He used his other hand to jerk her face back to his. He heard her breath catch, felt her body tremble. "I think, before we officially say goodbye, you'd want to make good on your integrity. I think you'd want things clean." He used his foot to nudge her ankle, untangling her legs. "Complete."

Fresh tears shimmered in her eyes. "Shit!" she muttered.

"What?" He pressed fully against her now. "What is it? What did I just push, Rose?"

She shoved at him. "What didn't you just push!" She shot up a stare that knifed him with its anguish. "Clean. You want *clean?* From me, Senator? Really? Have you Googled Rose Fabian lately? Lots of things pop up, I assure you. None of them even remotely means clean, complete, tidy, or simple."

"I never said I wanted simple."

"And I never committed to anything more than last night."

"Which is why you rewrote your parting shot fifteen times," he countered, "and then showed up in class looking like a shark chewed you up and spit you out." He jammed his hand into her hair now, refusing her any extra movement. "Last night was just a taste, and you loved it. You want this, pet. No, you need it. And you need it from me."

Her eyes darkened, and her nostrils flared. "You have no idea what I need."

He let out a black laugh. "Then enlighten me. Here's your forum, honey. I'm all ears." He screwed his hold tighter. Though she took a sharp breath, her nipples turned to gumdrops against her shirt. "*Talk*, Rose. Now!"

Her tongue darted over her lips, but then she reset her luscious mouth into a line. Her gaze, while raised to his, was cloaked behind a curtain of stubbornness.

"Damn it." He let his fury surge into the words. He'd hoped to go at this more civilized than he had last night, not knowing what her brother had said to make her flee this morning. But she was throwing up an emotional version of the goddamn Great Wall of China.

"Fine." He pushed back but kept his stare fixed to hers. "I don't take silence as a safe word. You won't talk, so instead you'll strip."

The sheen in her eyes turned to shock. "Excuse me?"

"That's not your safe word either. Do you remember your safe word, pet?"

A shudder claimed her body when he dropped the last word on her, even if it was a snarl. He watched, alternately fascinated and relieved, as her face began to transform, to soften. Christ, maybe yanking out his heavy Dom was really the key. Did she feel this as he beheld it? Was it possible that she still didn't understand how she was meant for the pleasure of D/s as much as he? That even a simple subbie endearment began changing her into this breathtaking creature, her head starting to bow, her whole body swaying toward him?

Why the hell was she walking away from something she so clearly wanted?

But more importantly, how was he going to change her mind?

The answer to that came as easy as his next breath. He'd do it by focusing everything he knew as a Dominant, and everything he felt as a man, into setting her free even more than before. Even better than before.

"O-Of course I remember my safe word."

Fuck. That hoarse edge to her voice just juiced him hotter. He leaned in again at her, cocking his head. "Of course I remember...what?"

"I remember, Sir."

He hummed in approval. She shook from head to toe. So goddamn sexy. "And are you using that safe word now?"

She darted her gaze away. He waited, holding his breath. If he lost her again, it might be now. He forced himself to wait through that taut wire of a moment, determining whether they'd keep heading for the horizon together or turn back for the shore—and the finality of her fear.

"No. I'm not using it, Sir."

Mark closed his eyes. "My beautiful, good girl. Thank you." He pressed a kiss to her forehead. "And now that we've got that squared away, you'll strip for me, please."

As he expected, that got her gaze back in line. "S-Sir?"

He couldn't help the wicked grin that tugged his lips. "Is the command confusing, Rose?"

"No, but—" She glanced at the big Bahamian who stood at the captain's wheel, his back to them. "You mean everything? Here?"

He dropped the smile. "Yes, pet. And now. Don't worry about Gervais. He's been screened, and he's the picture of discretion. He'll be keeping his eyes on the ocean." He cocked his head a little. "Unless you'd *like* him to watch?"

She glowered. "Are you trying to talk me into or out of this?"

He recrossed his arms. "I'm not talking with you at all. I'm ordering you, Rose. Clothes. Off. Everything. Now. You have thirty seconds. Anything that's not off by then, I'll tear and toss."

Her mouth opened again, as if she got ready to fire off another objection, but then he looked at his watch with raised brows. Her stunned little "Shit!" got muffled as she peeled off her shirt. The shorts got shucked just as fast.

"Time's up."

He stated it as she hooked her thumbs into the waist of her delectably virginal white thong. After a sharp look from him, she dropped her hands.

Mark didn't disguise his deep swallow. Christ, even nearly nude, his pet was breathtaking. The sunlight poured over her breasts like brandy. Her waist was a gentle, sexy curve. Her thighs were long, soft waves of curved grace. Her nipples puckered tighter beneath his rapt stare, and she bent her head again. The woman adopted a submissive's perfect stance with zero training.

She made him hard in seconds.

Certain she observed that fact with where her gaze dropped, he nonetheless scooted forward until his toes were outside hers. Without another word, he hooked his index fingers into both sides of her panties.

Tore.

Hard.

She gasped. The garment dropped, exposing the mahogany curls at the doorway of her pussy. He looked back up, past the breaths lifting her chest, to find her wide gaze waiting for him. Her eyes burned with copper lights, glowing against thick shadows of desire.

Mark let her see the lock of his teeth. "Pick the panties up," he directed. "But turn your back and spread your legs as you do. I want to see every crevice of the body that belongs to me right now."

He heard every succulent note of her full, answering gasp. As she blew it out, she pivoted to obey him. He growled as she leaned over, exposing the lips of her sex, a secret pink seashell for him.

"Walk to the rail," he directed. "And throw them in that trash barrel on the way. While you're there, add that hair tie too."

Once more, she complied with exquisite grace. He greedily stared his fill, his chest filled with pride and, yes, awe. She wasn't a waif-thin debutante or even a doctored-up supermodel, though she carried herself with twice the poise of the first and thrice the style of the second. Her body belonged to another time when men worshiped elegant curves like hers. He was extremely glad this wasn't a real pirate galleon, when he'd have to worry about a crew full of toothless Bluebeards who'd try to knife him to fuck her. It would've made him a mass murderer as well, because right now he'd gouge the balls off even a fly who tried to touch her.

By the time she'd tossed the wrecked panties and then set her hair free, turning it into a glorious russet banner in the wind, he'd moved up behind her. He clamped his hands over her wrists, fastening them down on the rail, while he fitted his lips against her ear. "Spread your legs again," he told her. "Wider. Move your body. Fit your ass to my cock. You can feel how hard it is, can't you? Do you feel what you do me, Rose?" An acquiescing whimper erupted out of her. He held himself still, squeezing his ass to lock himself in place as she rolled her hips and adjusted the soft globes of her backside against the pounding rod between his thighs. "Yessss. That's it. Very good, honey."

Her body quaked, but she undulated again, as mesmerizing as the waves beneath them. Mark matched her moves, blown away once more by how she fit so perfectly into him, almost losing himself to the magic of her—but they were a long way off from that. He realigned his head, the big one this time, to the purpose of why he'd secured her like this. He wanted her totally aware of him, surrounded by him bodily as he again tried to delve at her mentally.

"So, my pet, are you ready to talk now?"

"T-Talk?" She tensed. "I...I thought this was a punishment."

"Aren't they one and the same for you right now?"

"What's that supposed to— Ohhhh!"

He squeezed his fingers tighter over the breast he'd cupped. "All right, I'll even make it easier. I'll tell you exactly what we'll talk about." He pulled at her flesh, making her nipple stand out so he could tease its tender tip with his fingernail. "I know you got a phone call when I was out this morning. I know it was your brother."

Whatever she hadn't stiffened against him before, she did now. He almost chuckled. As if he'd let her get away with any resistance. She seemed to know that too, visibly warring between what her body wanted and her mind protested. "This isn't fair."

"Nor was what you did this morning."

"What I did this morning—"

"Was walk out without explanation, without a chance for us to talk, to work things through. You call that fair?"

Mark let go of her breast and latched his hand around her free wrist again. She still tried to wrestle. "There's nothing to work through. I just...can't do this!"

"Damn it." He snarled it against her neck. "When are you going to get it? I don't scare that fucking easily, Rose. I don't back down from the things I know are right. I won't walk away from the *people* I know are right. And I'm not walking away—"

"From me?"

Her retort was wrapped in such pure pain, he slackened from shock. Rose, clearly waiting for the reaction, took instant advantage by twisting free and turning around. At once, she rammed both palms to the center of his chest.

"I've got a command for *you* now," she snapped. "You need to walk." Another shove. "No, you need to run." One more. "I'm *not* the right thing, okay? I'm not the right person." She tried one more, but her arms went limp. "God! How many more ways do I have to say it? Please, just—"

Her face crunched. Her punches at his chest hadn't made a dent, but tears openly poured from her now. *Damn it.*

He was split wide open, heart and soul. He grabbed her wrists again, forcing aside his fury at her brother, at least from the ferocity of his physical hold. Yet when he spoke, all holds were off—and his rage was very much *on*.

"What the hell did he say to you? What the *hell* did that bastard do to your head now?"

She shook her head, crying harder.

"Rose. Goddamn it!" The curse tore up from his gut, a sound as raw as her sobs. He hauled her against him, clawing a hand at the back of her head. "Talk to me!"

He felt her breathing quicken, the words practically clamoring to get out of her. But when all she gave over was a frustrated huff, he pried her arms loose. Tore back from her.

His way was thoroughly clear.

His purpose was clearly defined.

If she wasn't going to break down her wall, he'd tear it apart, brick by fucking brick.

"I'm sorry." The words spilled from her on hollow chokes. They tore him deeper than her tears, though he scourged himself for not expecting them. Clearly she took his action as a final kiss-off—and naturally, she stumbled toward the puddles of her clothes. "I knew I shouldn't have done this. I didn't want it to come to this. I didn't want to fail you. *Shit*. I...I didn't want to care like this..."

"Stop." He flung out his arm, his hand splayed like a damn superhero trying to stop a train. The comparison sure fit when it came to this woman. "Don't you dare take another step. That is a huge fucking order."

Her responding gape, along with her fast obedience, gave him deep satisfaction. And a rush of lust.

He stomped up the steps to the upper deck. A bank of shroud ropes waited there. The interlocked hemp ladders, fanning down from the main mast, were supposedly there just for the yo-ho-ho prop effect on the yacht. Yeah, right. The second he'd seen them this afternoon, plans had sprung for more interesting uses, if things came to that.

They'd come to that.

He swung an expectant stare back down at Rose. "*Now* you can move. Scoot your apologetic little ass up here, in front of me. You have thirty seconds again, woman, and they started five seconds ago."

She was a delectable combination of frantic and sexy as she scurried, slid, and bounced up the stairs, gaining enough speed to crash into him upon arrival. Mark steadied her by grabbing her shoulders, tempted to let his hands pick up a pace of their own and glide right over her creamy breasts. But he knew that in minutes, those swells were going to be his to own and play with anyway.

He could wait...

Maybe.

Damn, *damn*, she was resplendent. Her cheeks, flushed from the wind, were kissed by thick tendrils of her hair. Her gaze reflected the sky, the sun's umber glow mixing with the dark-chocolate depths threatening, as always, to pull him in and drown him alive.

He steeled his composure. Redoubled his focus. Now wasn't the time for letting *her* drown *him*. There was only one way he was going to save this gift for which they'd both searched so hard and waited so long. Now was the time to plunge deep and pull out the Dominant who hadn't seen the light of day for a while, a creature who hadn't gotten out a lot even during his years with Heather. Huge reason for that. This side of him really was a twisted Bluebeard. But if the occasion—and the submissive—called for his heavier hand of kink, he'd bring it to the damn party. With pleasure.

"Still nothing to say?" He let the guy out slowly at first, letting him murmur the words while curving a possessive hand around her elbow. When he tightened his grip a little more, Rose dipped her head lower, an acknowledgment of his command. He looked at her head, baffled. So brave, so strong when it came to giving him her body, but Fort Knox about exposing anything else. Why?

He wasn't getting off this damn vessel until he found out.

He pulled her toward the shrouds. "All right. On the ropes, face up. Spread yourself for me, arms and legs. The lines are secure and the angle isn't steep; you won't have trouble balancing." He raised his brows at her wince of hesitation. "Is there an issue with my instructions, pet?"

She visibly trembled again at his last word. "You...you want me facing you?"

Mark cupped her cheek. "Oh yes, Rose. You're going to face me. I'm going to watch you. I'm going to read you. If you won't speak to me with your lips, you'll speak to me with your body. I'm going to know every twitch, every reaction, every sensation you feel. I'm going to absorb it all."

He let that sink into her psyche. It was erotic as hell to watch, her features betraying her inner struggle between *Oh God yes, watch me please* and a catty version of *We'll fucking see about that.* She was so damned enticing that he could've studied her for another hour—if he didn't know what was coming next. That lent him the strength to pull his hand back, letting her hustle into position as he pivoted toward a nearby gear locker.

The box he opened was marked *Tackle and Hooks*, could've still been the truth if that equipment was hiding under the bondage and discipline gear on top. He grinned, remembering

Gervais's pride when showing him the box during the vessel tour this afternoon. Maybe it was a special request the man got more often than Mark assumed. Whatever the reason, he was damn delighted for the treasure trove, a conclusion backed by his inner Bluebeard as he ran a hand along the items...

And formed a lesson plan for his stubborn little subbie.

Her unexpected intractability had forced him to considerably tweak things. He had to anticipate a true fight from her now. He would really have to turn the punishment over to the pirate.

He would have to keep thinking with the head atop his shoulders, no matter how hard the clamor got from the one between his thighs.

"Hell."

He muttered that as soon as he turned back. His cock already challenged him on his resolution, reacting at once to the sight of his spread-eagle submissive. She was a fantasy come to life. Her hair flowed to either side of her wide-eyed face. The silk of her skin contrasted with her coarse rope bed, and he already imagined the patterns that would form across her back, thighs, and ass. And ohhhh, how he planned to mark the front of her chest, arms, and thighs...

As his mind spun the thought into some amazing images of erotic art, his erection pounded at his zipper. *Control it. Control it. Think about the old days, maybe. A budget bill. A droning filibuster. Congressional minutes to review.*

No dice. The torment got no better as he moved to her without a word, four lengths of red-dyed rope in his grip. He'd almost opted for the ease of spring cords, but this occasion called for a more primeval theme. She'd sealed that decision when she all but dared him to jam his hand down her throat and haul the words out of her. He moved with gruff concentration, deciding on easy buntline ties, rechecking the knots to make sure they were secure but not tight.

With every new knot he tied, he watched Rose's reaction. This was going to be a different bondage experience for her. The sexy foreplay of last night wasn't part of tonight's roster. Nor was she going to get his kisses, his adoration, his seduction. She seemed to understand that, if he judged right from her lowered eyes and the serious set of her mouth. But he was resolved to doing much more than guessing at her mindset. He wanted inside her, *all* of her, and the communication of that goal started right now.

With the resolve coursing his veins, he cinched the last knots around her ankles. He watched her arms and thighs flex, testing the bonds. He hadn't left much wiggle room, another silent sign to her, one he expected resistance for. But she stunned him yet again, her body going lax, her head lolling against the nets.

Christ. Was the tight captivity *pleasant* for her? Was his little Rose even more a natural submissive than he presumed?

The next moment brought his confirmation. Her eyes slid closed. Her breasts, while still sprouting the most erect nipples he'd ever seen, rose and fell on longer, deeper breaths. And her pussy...

Fuck.

He couldn't hold back from dipping a finger into the moist curls at her center. For the first time since they'd boarded the boat, she gave a full-throated cry.

"Such a wet little cunt already." He pressed his chest to hers, rolling a thumb along her clit. "Once again, racing on without permission."

"I'm sorry, Sir." Her voice dropped to a breathy gasp. "I couldn't help it."

"Of course you couldn't, honey." He trailed from her ear to her mouth with the tip of his tongue, making her shake and sob again. "But now that we've established how much your body yearns to be with me, it's time we find out why your head keeps telling you otherwise. More importantly...about the bastard who's been fucking with it."

He punctuated that by withdrawing his fingers, moving to her sweet mound. He palmed her there with fierce possession.

"I'd ask if you're ready, pet, but it doesn't matter. Here we go, whether you like it or not."

CHAPTER SIXTEEN

Damn. *Damn.*

Rose battled to hang on to the sanity of the word, to the coherent thought it took to form it, even silently. What the hell had happened to her? Three minutes ago, she'd listened to the man talk with the arrogance of a Dom dentist, planning to hit her with some magical kink Novocain and extract what he needed out of her head. She'd almost laughed at him. She'd definitely scoffed. Not where he could see her do it of course, but it wasn't like she didn't know what he could do to her. Mark had taken her to sexual and spiritual heaven more times in the last twenty-four hours than she ever dreamed possible. She knew what he could do with restraints, with words, and with those incredible, knowing hands of his. But she could handle all of that now. Maybe he really didn't know how adept she could be at turning off parts of herself at will—even when the On button was him.

But that was just the problem.

He...wasn't himself anymore.

Apparently the man had a different person stashed in that box he'd been sifting through. This Mark had the same carved golden torso, warrior's stance, and precise confidence of the lover she *thought* she knew—but one look at his face told her differently.

This person was an illumination. His eyes burned with a strange new fire. His jaw was so taut it redefined the shape of his face. He'd transformed beyond her teacher, her lover, her Dominant. She seriously pondered if some merciless pirate had resurrected from the hold and taken possession of him.

She also wondered why the hell that turned her pussy into a floodgate.

And her mind into this wasteland.

She searched the blackness behind her eyelids, attempting to get centered again. Maybe if she just didn't look at him...

"Open your eyes, pet." The directive was pure granite but backed by a velvety caress to her face. It wasn't his hand but something just as persuasive. "No drifting. Eyes right here, on your Master."

Master. She loved the sound of that—and yeah, he probably knew it. Attempting a steady breath, she complied. Well...tried to. Her heartbeat went AWOL as she beheld him, more pirate-like than ever now that twilight had fallen, stroking the leather falls of a sizable flogger. Okay, so it *seemed* sizable. She wasn't in a position to compare, as her few trips to Fallon's favorite kink club had been more about watching the effects of floggers on subs, rather than the instruments themselves. Those memories, joined with the preview Mark had given her of *this* flogger, had her brain and her body duking it out for possession of her composure.

"Shit!" It spilled without thought. Mark—or whoever he was now—barely reacted beyond a satisfied glow in his eyes. Was he enjoying this? These things inflicted pain! She remembered that much. Vividly. And she wasn't—

"*Shit!*"

This time, the word popped out more from astonishment, coinciding with the first stroke he inflicted. He'd barely moved his wrist to lay the falls across her thighs. Her skin warmed and then tingled. She took a deep breath, relaxing for a second.

All right, that wasn't so bad. A bit pleasant, even.

It was also a beginner's tap.

"No more words." He emphasized with a second *thwack*, backed by more muscle. Oh, this one stung, but Rose clenched back her retort, bolting a glare into him instead as he finished, "You'll get to use words when I direct them from you. Understood?"

As she debated how to best narrow her eyes more, he dipped his last word into a seductive murmur...brushing her exposed labia with the leather strands.

Dear. God.

She squeezed her eyes shut. The moan in her throat turned into a choke.

"Y-Yes, Sir."

Smack.

He replaced the falls with his palm and not nearly with as much tenderness. Her eyes flew open. Had he just *spanked* her pussy? And—*shit*—was her vagina drenched in reaction?

"Very sweet and respectful, honey—but not the words I'm waiting to hear."

He stepped closer, the wicked light in his eyes searching for something in hers. Apparently he found it, because his lips twisted into a confident smirk—right before he palmed her sex again. "We'll get to the words. Don't you worry. Right now, you've agreed to accept a punishment for turning tail on your Master this morning. You're going to feel a little of what it was like in my heart, to realize you didn't trust me enough to stay and face me."

"No!" It burst before she could stop it, fueled by watching him swing the flogger in more ferocious swoops. "It's not you!

I've trusted you with everything!"

He laughed. Sort of. "More words. More bullshit I don't want to hear. Keep it up, Rose, and your welts will be as blue as this ocean by the time we're done."

"But you need to understand. You need to—"

"*Silence!*"

His bellow came with a frightening *thwack* of the flogger to the deck near her feet. In the aftermath, she looked on as Mark heaved on his breaths, gritting his teeth, watching her with feral appraisal. Rose shook violently, but her terror suddenly had nothing to do with what he was going to do with her. Shit. *Shit!* All his actions were a terrible revelation, showing her what she'd done to him, how deep the cut she'd truly inflicted by walking out this morning. She'd had no idea. She'd thought he'd call her a few choice things, have the bed changed, and then subject her to an emotional blackout for the rest of the week.

She'd never thought he'd feel this...pain. Over her.

She'd never thought she'd cause *anyone* pain like this. Ever.

Her brain unleashed an ocean of misery on her heart.

She raised her head, hoping he'd look up just once—and see how she knew now.

How she *knew.*

How she was so sorry for what she'd done...

But through the first dozen blows, his focus seemed only on the body he disciplined. He said nothing else. The air was filled with his raging grunts, the ominous whirs of the falls, the hard *thwacks* on her skin, and her deep, resigned silence. Even as the blows got harder, Rose swallowed and held back her screams. The flogger's bites were whispers of pain compared to the sorrow in her soul.

I'm sorry. Oh, Sir...so sorry.

He finally looked at her face. He did it only for a moment, after turning to shake his hair free of sweat. A flash of disbelief darkened his eyes before he whooshed the flogger high again.

Despite her resolve, the strike made her cry out. He'd been targeting the flesh of her thighs and arms, so the blow across her breasts was a sharp shock. The flesh there was already puckered and sensitive because of the wind. His strike filled them with sudden stings.

But then she got the real stunner. To compensate for the pain, she tried to twist her hips. The ropes didn't let her move much, but far enough that when her pussy shifted, those wet lips kissed each other in more than a few places.

Arousal flared up her body. Her outcry was quickly drowned by her hiss.

She looked back to Mark.

Again, he was a man transformed.

Raw power filled every angle of his face. His lips, slightly parted, twisted with victory. Cords stood out in his neck. Veins were prominent in his chest and biceps.

For a long moment, she forgot about being sorry, stubborn, or anything except totally turned on.

He wielded the flogger again, once more aiming across her thighs—only this time, riveting his stare on hers too. And bunching his arm hard with the effort.

This time, it really hurt.

Rose shrieked—but forgot the pain in the very same moment, watching what her shudders and writhing did to him. He dragged in a harsh breath. The corners of his eyes twitched. His free hand shifted to his crotch, nursing the growing ridge there.

She barely had time to catch her breath before he laid the falls again across her breasts. Again harder than before. Again forcing her to twist her hips. Again sending the pulses through her pussy, her body, clear into her scalp. Her lips parted on another hiss. His jaw clenched.

The pattern began.

His flogger strike. Her scream.

His caught breath. Her rolling hips.

Their growing, connected need. Their spiraling, mutual desire. Sting and succor. Pain and pleasure. A place far beyond where they'd been together last night. A man different than the Dominant who'd taken her in the storm by the pool and then seduced her in his bed. This merciless pirate wasn't going to do any of that. His whole face told her so. When his body joined with hers, it was going to be brutal, primal.

And God help her, she couldn't wait.

And damn it, she knew he recognized that too.

As if seeing the thought take over her mind, Mark hurled the flogger to the deck and then regained the space between them. Instead of pressing his body against her like he had before, he grabbed the shrouds beneath her, pulling her against his body. He had her fully surrounded, completely bound.

His to be used.

She whimpered, only hoping his need was worse than hers and he'd be inside her soon, no more questions asked. They'd have this last beautiful bonding here on the sea, where they were safe from the world. Maybe, for a little while longer, her fantasy would be safe from Shane's reality.

"All right, honey. *Now* we're going to talk."

She groaned. So much for wishes coming true. "What?

Why?" She tried to plead it into his lips, to take advantage of the heavy lust that clearly plagued him as much as her. But he shook his head, fanning his heated breath across her face.

"Not an approved response." He pulled again on the ropes. The action brought her spread mound against the rough bulge of his crotch. "Give me what I need, and you'll get what you need."

Her right wrist flinched, reacting to the instinct to slap him. She huffed, knowing she'd have a rope burn now from the effort.

"No need to get testy." He made the shrouds sway a little so every inch of her pussy got a rolling tease from his erection. "The question is easy, pet. Just tell me, damn it. What did your brother call you about?"

"Shiiiit!" She sucked in ragged air. Her whole pelvis shook. "Oh Sir...that feels so..."

"Not approved either." He eased back on the ropes. She could feel her labia convulsing, her clit trembling. Every nerve between her thighs screamed for release. He couldn't be doing much better, despite the iron control in his voice. "You know what *is* approved for discussion. Shane. You. This morning." He rolled his hips, ruthlessly taunting her with a crotch-to-crotch flyby. "Was it about me?"

Rose reacted instinctively, jerking her gaze from him.

Mark palmed her cheek, forcing her to look back. "Nail on the fucking head, huh?"

"H-How do you even know his name?"

"What did he want to know about me?"

"Mark." Tears hovered in her entreaty. "Sir. Please—"

"He told you to sleep with me, didn't he?"

A weepy laugh spilled out. "God! And you think I ran

because of that? You think I left *you* just to piss him off?" She struggled to look away again, but his grip didn't relent. "Damn it, stop! It's more complicated than that!"

"Okay. He told you *not* to sleep with me."

"All Shane did was talk some sense into me, all right? Does that make you feel better now? Are you satisfied?"

His hold relaxed, but his voice hardened. "That's it. I'm completely right. He drilled right in and got to you. That bastard punched all his old shit right back into your head, crap he's been feeding you for years, even before Owen. He probably told you about being no good for me, to stay away and not corrupt the good senator with your eccentric reputation and your depraved sexual tendencies. No, wait. He didn't stop there, did he? He likely found a great way to call you five kinds of alley cat too, right? Forget the 'black sheep of the family' shit. That's much too easy for an asshole like him."

"Stop! Please, just stop!" She drew a hard breath, getting ready to say it. *Worth.* The irony of all ironies. A safe word that embodied the furthest thing she felt right now.

"No." It was a vicious syllable, spoken in the moment he captured hers in a fierce, fervent kiss. "No, goddamn it, we're not stopping. Shane's wrong, Rose. He couldn't be more wrong." With her face still pinned by his mouth, he slid his arms along hers, locking their hands, fitting his body atop hers with a thrust of undeniable intent. "To start with, I'd challenge him to name exactly who's been corrupting who here..."

"Ohhhh, shit!" She moaned it as he dropped his head down to her breast. "Oh!" she cried again as he bit one of her nipples like it was an exotic, tender piece of fruit. He closed a hand over her other breast, teasing that engorged nub with his thumb.

"Or," he continued, growling seductively as he withdrew something from one of his pockets, "whether there's been damn near enough corruption going on."

Rose tried to see what new toy had turned his voice back into that pirate's tone and had his cock swelling anew against her mound, but he took the sneak attack approach. Before she determined what the cold, steel pressure was on the underside of her breasts, he had the clamps fastened to her nipples.

"Ohhhh, *Sir*!"

Mark devoured the rest of her scream with his mouth, looming over her, grasping her hair, and groaning into her in return. When he released her, there was a smile—a damn *smile*!—on his lips. "My good pet. How fun it is to corrupt you." He stroked the outside of her breasts. "You're so goddamn gorgeous like this."

She yearned to scream again. To order him to pull them off. The pain was hideous at first, two crunches of consuming agony, but then she listened to his voice. His sensual praise made it easy to breathe through the first minute. The way he stroked her flesh, moving his hands down her body by heated inches, made the second and third minutes easier. When he got his hands around her ass, kneading her cheeks so her sex slid perfectly against his crotch, she nearly forgot about the clamps. Every sensation in her body was eclipsed by the rising, burning need in her soaked, throbbing pussy.

"Sir." She made it a plea, her voice high and breathy. "Sir, please! I need..."

"Yes, honey." He jerked at his pants now, the rip of his zipper like a glorious angels' chorus on the sea wind. "I know what you need." His erection burst free, the moist head demanding a path through her curls, seeking her intimate sheath. He took out a condom packet from his pocket, ripped it open with his teeth, and rolled it on with a low groan.

As he angled his hips and lined himself up with her vagina, he brushed the hair from her face and hovered his mouth over hers. "I'm going to fuck you hard, Rose—and I hope your goddamn brother hears you screaming all the way back in Chicago."

She smiled and gave a teary nod to that. The next instant, she wondered if he really did intend her shriek to be heard in Chicago. As he drove his cock into her core, he gave the attaching chain to her clamps a sharp tug. Adrenaline charged her system, turning her senses into a fireworks show, and she ignited, breaking open with need. It was the most agonizing and amazing physical experience she'd ever had. Her head slammed back. She wrenched her eyes shut. Her senses spun and burned as she struggled to process it all at once.

"That's it." Mark's voice came filled with equal parts desire and demand. "Accept it. Take it. The pain is making it better for you. You knew that when I was marking you with the flogger, didn't you? You felt it in the deepest parts of your cunt, how you opened and accepted more of the pleasure after you took the pain. This part is even better. Breathe, baby. Open up to it. Open up to me and all the good things this can be for you."

She nodded again, though the motion was shaky. He began moving inside her now, sliding his hard, huge length to the very edge of her pussy lips and then thrusting back in with deliberate rhythm. "Do you feel this, honey? Do you feel the head of my cock, about to kiss your sweet spot inside...here?"

She gasped as he gave an extra little push, the tip of his cock indeed hitting a spot in her tunnel that made her start to quake from the inside out. "Oh, God!" she cried out. "Yes!"

"And does your ass feel my hot balls as I fuck you deeper... like this?"

"Yes." She panted and sighed. "Yes, yes, yesssss."

"And does your sweet little asshole feel my finger playing with it, exploring it, turning you on more...like this?"

Her head began to swim, her body disengaging from reality. "Ohhhh yes, Sir..."

"And will you trust me for the rush again, letting me pull your clamps off, letting you hurt some more again for me...like this?"

"Fuck!" Her back arched off the nets as the blood rushed back to her nipples in a torturous rush. Her whole body tightened. She felt her walls clamp around Mark's driving, penetrating stalk. He swelled and surged against her, and his balls contracted beneath their joined bodies.

"Oh, yeah." He gripped her hips to drive the pace, setting a relentless beat. "Let it take you over, pet. Let it explode through you. You're going to come now, and I'm going to come with you. Now, Rose. *Now!*"

Her body didn't need another word. Her senses flew, soaring on the wind, spiraling for the clouds. Then she careened even past that, her senses rocketing for the stars, her body bursting in a supernova of ecstasy. She felt every pulse of his shaft as he rammed into her and then froze, exploding deep in her body on a guttural, primal groan.

Many minutes later, still buried inside her, Mark deposited tender kisses on her closed eyelids, prompting her into a soft little hum. She finally opened her eyes to find his face bathed in starlight, his gaze aglow with curiosity.

"Okay...what are you thinking?"

A furrow invaded his brow. The next moment, he smiled

it away. "I'll share after you're untied and I get some Vitamin E oil into your skin."

"Promise?"

He wrote in the air with one finger. "In permanent marker."

CHAPTER SEVENTEEN

Forty-five minutes later, Mark used the finger with which he'd written his air assurance to follow a more interesting path, the swell of his submissive's lovely ass.

He'd taken Rose down into the yacht's sumptuous stateroom, getting her aftercare started immediately, wiping her down with eucalyptus-scented cloths and then massaging the oils infused with lavender and Vitamin E into her skin. After that, he'd brushed the tangles from her hair, relishing the chance to have every strand of that mahogany mane in his hands.

Now she was stretched across the soft coverlet of the big bed with him, stomach down, head resting on her folded arms, quietly looking on as he traced the crisscross rope burns across her creamy skin.

"Does it look nice?" she asked softly.

He chuckled. "Ohhh yes, honey." He gulped hard as he followed one very low, down into the crevice between her ass cheeks. "Beautiful."

Her lips inched up. "It feels beautiful."

"You sure about that?" He trailed his finger up to one of her eyebrows, looking into the thoughtful brown depths in the gaze below it. Her smile hadn't extended there.

"Oh, I'm sure." Her tone reminded him of her don't-doubt-me comeback from the first day they met.

"Then what is it?"

She worried her bottom lip with her teeth. "I don't just feel beautiful here. I felt beautiful...out there too. On the deck, when you had me tied down. Even when it hurt. Perhaps... *especially* when it hurt. It brought something out in you that made me feel amazing. Desired." She rolled to her side, facing him now but not looking right at him. "As if we were purging demons or something." A nervous spurt tumbled out of her. "That's ridiculous, isn't it?"

Mark pulled her close and captured her lips. "Not at all," he whispered. "It's completely possible."

She lifted her mouth to his again, a silent entreaty for that contact, and he gave it to her with passionate fullness. Her mouth welcomed him just like her body had, with soft supplication and warm surrender. She let him fill her up again, possessing her with his tongue, but that was the grand-slam paradox of the night. The truth was, *she* filled *him*. He never thought he'd be complete or understood again. Her brave confession had just topped him off. He was officially at the brim, and he showed her that by wrapping his arm around her waist, deepening their embrace. When they pulled apart, they didn't go very far. Their breaths mingled against the pillows, their bodies fitted...two broken pieces, fixed by being one.

That thought, enormous and sudden, made him sit up. He managed to look casual about the movement, reaching for a bottle of water on the nightstand. "Here." He extended the bottle to Rose. "You need to keep hydrating, pet."

"Thanks." She quirked a little grin. "Uh...I think."

She looked at him with open inquisition, but Mark rose, evading that silent query. She was likely going to ask if he was okay, and he didn't know that answer. He needed a few minutes to clear the debris of the mental detonation. He realized it had first hit him out on deck, when he'd still been balls-deep inside her. It struck again now with more brutal impact.

Shit.

It couldn't really be...

Could it?

"Are you hungry?" He stroked her cheek after tugging his shirt back on. "Gervais has some food ready up top. Throw on a robe and join me."

When she reappeared on deck a few minutes later, sending another explosion through him just by showing up in the fluffy white robe, he'd reconciled himself to the truth that now glared through his being. But what kind of words went with this? How did he say it? There was no way around it. The bomb had gone off at full strength. But that was the thing about dynamite. *It* found *you*. And its timing was always usually piss-poor.

"This is amazing." Rose breathed it as she gazed out over the water, where the moon made a silver necklace on the waves and the lights of Nassau formed a rainbow ribbon in the distance. He took in her profile, so classic and timeless, again wondering if he weren't going to be flung back in time once he spoke his next words.

"I'm falling in love with you."

Her face snapped toward him. Her lips parted, but no sound came out.

"No. Strike that." He leaned forward, palming her cheek. "I've already fallen. And I don't want you to go to Baghdad. I want you by my side, here, forever." A sheen appeared in her deep velvet gaze, and he rushed on. "I know, I know; it's only been five days. But we've spent more time together even now than most couples—"

"I love you too."

She pressed her hand over his as tears dragged down her cheeks.

"You do?"

She nodded. But that didn't ease the fist in his gut.

"Then why don't those look like tears of joy, honey?"

"Because this—us—still can't happen."

He pulled back his hand. And forced it not to form a fist. "All right," he said from taut lips. "I'm listening."

"Don't be mad." She threaded her fingers back into his. "You don't think I want to tell Gervais to turn this thing around and set a one-way course to Jamaica? But that would be no better for you than I am, Mark."

Fuck calm and controlled. He pushed her hand away before lurching to his feet. "God*damn* it! Really? Are we back to that?"

Her resigned slump did nothing to assuage him. "First of all, I've made a commitment to the project and to the team."

"Which you can still fulfill, in other capacities, as a domestically based consultant."

She pursed her lips. He was right, and she knew it. "More to the point then, I refuse to drag you into the public mess of my reputation."

"Because of Tristan Rouselle's bid for my vacant senate seat?"

Her shocked blinks were only a click better than the funereal mope. "You know about that?"

He nodded tersely. "I snapped it together the second I found out who your brother is. I figured that was why he called you, as well."

She coiled her hands in her lap. "The call was well-timed,

despite the reason." She glanced up. Rolled her eyes. "Please don't glare at me like that—"

"I'm going to do more than glare at that bastard."

"Mark—"

He slashed a hand. "Let me take a stab at this. He probably started with the age gap. Then he went for the difference in our backgrounds and our social circles. Let's see... What other shit did the prick uncover?"

"Stop!" She jerked to her feet, her spine stiff as the ship's mast. "It has nothing to do with any of that, okay?" She brought up a hand to his shoulder. Her touch was insistent but gentle. "All those things...I have to admit that at first, I brought them up myself." She shook her head, chuffing softly. "What silly arguments. I know my heart now. It treasures yours, whether you're a senator, a sailor, a millionaire, or a mine worker; and whether you're nineteen or ninety..."

"*Ninety?*"

They both chuckled at his quip. But the sadness reentered her eyes all too quickly. "Mark, my Sir...I adore you. I love you. But I'll fail you."

He grabbed her hand off his shoulder, squeezing it. "Probably," he answered. "More than once. That's what happens in relationships, honey. Guess what? Unlike that boy who almost ruined you for life, I can handle it."

Her features twisted. "Even when the whole world's watching?" When he took the chance to roll his eyes, she tugged back at his hand. "We *have* to think about this. You've worked too hard for your integrity, Mark. You've helped people. You're still helping them. When I fuck things up, when I don't get it right, what will they think?"

He laughed softly. "That we're both human?"

"Yeah, right. What they'll see is a head-in-the-clouds eccentric who's thrown herself at a desperate older guy—"

"A *happy* older guy." He pulled her close, taking her lips in an urgent kiss. "Happy and not giving a fuck about what they all think." Tenderly, he stroked a thumb across her cheek, wiping the moisture there. She kept peering at him, looking so small and innocent in her robe, a startling contrast to the naked siren who'd pulled his soul from him an hour ago. "And oh yeah, ready to kick their collective asses for ogling his woman's ass while her head's preoccupied with the clouds."

That got her to give him a bittersweet little giggle. He longed to kiss her again but didn't. She took a deep breath, readying herself to say more. Things he wasn't going to like.

"I love you even more for wanting to slay all the dragons. But not when it's me who's responsible for setting them loose. Not when I'm the disaster."

"*Rose.*"

"Don't." She pushed away and went to the railing, gripping it with white knuckles. "Let's treasure what we've had, okay? Let me go, Mark."

He longed to go to her again. To yank her right off her bejeweled feet and crush her close as he kissed her until she couldn't breathe. But he needed to let her feel the power of his intent from right where he stood. "I've told you, damn it; I don't give up that easily."

Her fists coiled tighter on the rail. "And I'm asking you to be stronger than yourself. To understand this is for the best. I know what I'm saying sounds insane—"

"You're not insane!"

Fuck it. He did go to her, pressing himself against her, wrapping his arms and hands atop hers. "You're *not* insane, damn it. You're just wrong."

Though she fitted herself into him, her body tensed. The breeze caught her hair, wrapping it around his jaw. He inhaled deeply. She smelled like vanilla and wind and sex, making him close his eyes, knowing he had only a few minutes left to memorize this. The ocean twinkled before them, a starlit carpet spreading to the coastline in the distance. He hated that strip of glaring pastel already. It was a reminder of the real world—and the words she was about to say.

"I love you, Mark Moore. Which is why I'm asking you to let me sail away now too."

A million responses sprang to his mind other than the hard grunt he did give. He could tell her it was too damn late to accommodate her request. He could explain how he'd been dealt the worst DNA to deal with on this, the mate-for-life gene blended with the tenacity-to-the-point-of-stupidity trait. But he had a feeling she knew both already. She confirmed that with her next words, spoken with soft deliberation.

"It can't all be a cruise into forever, even when you long for it. Some journeys in our lives only last as long as the wind...a sigh of time. That's what makes sighs special. We have to treasure them for the beauty of their moments, *in* their moments, before they're carried away."

She stunned him yet again, with her poem-worthy words describing such a crap-ass truth. He turned her in his arms and lifted her face to him, even if his breath got sucked from his body in the doing. Even glimmering with the rivers of her tears, her skin was flawless cream. Her chin, her cheeks, and her forehead were etched in proud perfection. The russet fans of her lashes framed those eyes he'd never bottom out in but longed to try. He clenched his fists until they shook to prevent himself from reaching out to run his fingers over all of her, to help him remember, to engrave her into his psyche for the thousands of shitty, solitary nights ahead. He couldn't do it. If he did, this resolve would crumble, and he'd never let go.

"I love you," she repeated, her voice steady this time. "And that's why I refuse to ruin you."

"I know." The threads of acceptance in his tone made their way up his throat on fourteen-gauge needles of grief. "I... know."

★ ★ ★

The next day, it poured again. And though Mark yearned to bribe the clouds into sticking around as drinking buddies for his shit-ass mood, they moved on to more cheerful destinations, like the Bermuda Triangle. He put on a decent face for the world, but Dasha saw right through it, picking up on his gloom within minutes at breakfast. That afternoon, she texted to say she "really enjoyed Nassau" and was going to "hang out" for a few days to explore with David and Kress. Mark didn't buy her excuse for a second, but having her near made things just a fraction more bearable.

The sunshine and tropical breezes returned, taunting him with their glory like the Joker had joined forces with Gidget. The only relief he found to it all was one sight alone. Mahogany hair. Velvet eyes. Full lips. She always chose the back of the classroom now though was just as focused as she'd been day one. She still arrested his senses as she had on that day too. His cream-skinned dream. His misplaced Victorian.

His.

His.

Not her choice. Not their time.

Not to be.

He couldn't wait to get the hell off this island.

He arrived early to the jet GRI had chartered for the group back to Chicago. A lunch spread was ready and waiting in the spacious living room area of the plane, but he barely looked at the food. He headed straight for the back of the leather seating rows, spreading out the paperwork that formed an implied *Disturb Me At Your Own Risk* sign. Even Dasha read the message loud and clear, giving him a simple wave and a sympathetic smile as she, David, and Kress, having decided to hitch a ride back to the States with the group, boarded next. They staked out seats near the front, sharing a row with Brandt, who'd gotten erased off Pennington and Moridian's shit list the second he told them about the girlfriend back in Houston with whom he was "more obsessed than a cobra on a mongoose." They joined in the chatter as everyone else filed on board.

Everyone, Mark noted, except Rose.

He kept his head low and his face set when she finally made it, refusing to acknowledge how her arrival changed the very air in the cabin. All too easily his senses picked out the magnolias and vanilla in her scent alone. It would pass, he told himself. Just another second and the craving to leap up and claim her would be a dull twinge instead of a goddamn torment. It would pass.

He was also counting on her sitting anywhere but across the aisle.

He glanced up as she lowered into the seat and gave him an apologetic shrug. She was the last to board, so the seat was her only option. Mark returned an understanding smile and then let it drop as he looked back to the cancer research grant upon which he pretended to concentrate.

It was going to be a long goddamn flight.

Sure enough, the miles came to be marked by every sound, movement, and word from the woman across the aisle. There weren't many of all three. Against every order from his head otherwise, he constantly looked up to make sure Rose even continued to breathe. Every time, he found her the same: head dipped over her e-reader as if someone had written a modern-day Bible.

At the hundredth time he checked on her, he encountered a different view.

She was looking at *him*.

Intently. Unashamedly.

He savored the moment like a death row convict to a reprieve. The thick depths of her eyes, the love in her face, the submission in her smile...they filled him anew, like recognizing air all over again, reminding him of who he was. Her Dom. Her man. They'd part soon, separated by miles instead of feet, but this perfect sigh of a moment wasn't going to change. *Ever.*

It should have eased the ache. Instead his muscles fired with the need to move. Managing to keep the flames from the juncture of his thighs, he snapped free his seat belt and rose. He didn't release Rose's gaze. He didn't dare. He stepped in toward her, right past the boundaries of professional decorum, until they were dangerous inches apart.

He scooped her hand into his own and smiled softly. "Hi."

Her face glowed. His chest swelled with the satisfaction of causing it. "Hello there."

"Can I get you some food? You haven't eaten at all today, have you?"

That was the moment the spell broke. She remembered. She let reality crash back in on them. Mark gripped her tighter, willing her to stay on the cloud with him, but she yanked free. "I...I don't think so." She pulled her own seat belt free and pushed past him. "I think I just need to throw some water on my face."

She disappeared into the bathroom like a teen busted with pot. He would've snickered at the comparison if he didn't feel like her supplier.

Or totally sure about rolling up a bigger hit for them both.

He closed the distance to the bathroom door with an economy of movement. Everyone was too busy enjoying their last round of cocktails on GRI's dime, as well as a camera phone fest with Dasha, to notice him anyway. Standing at the door and bracing both hands to the portal, he leaned and listened. Running water. Frantic splashes. His little sub fuming at herself, probably intending to stay holed up in there for the rest of the flight.

For once, her retreat instinct was just fine with him.

He checked the door, hoping to find the green Vacant dot. A triumphant smirk spread across his face. She'd been too frantic to secure the lock. Fate had thrown him a bone.

She jerked up her horror-stricken face as he slid the door open and then sidestepped into the tight compartment. "What're you—"

"Ssshh." He jammed the lock home behind him. With his other hand, he grabbed a paper towel and pressed it to her face.

"This space isn't made for two pe—"

He wiped the towel across her lips. "It is now." He continued his ministration across her opposite cheek. When he concluded, he tossed the towel into the sink, picking up the excess water on her face with his mouth. "Honey," he murmured with heavy meaning. "You're all wet."

"Oh." It was more a sigh than anything, vibrating with the shiver that claimed her. "Yes. I suppose so."

He'd taken this risk with half an expectation of getting his face slapped and his ass shoved back out the door. Instead, she gave him the sweetest shock of the week. He let it make him bold, pushing even closer, trailing his lips into her hairline. Her gasp escalated into a sexier-than-hell moan, and she drew the sound out as he descended the column of her neck. Lightning had hit the plane now, he was sure of it, and the jolt went straight for his cock. He let out a growl to match her passion as he raised his head again, losing himself in the velvet depths of her eyes.

"Are you wet everywhere, pet?" He asked it as he gathered both her wrists into one of his hands, securing them at the small of her back. He started up her thigh with his other hand, fishing beneath her skirt for the treasure of her sweet, hot core. She started to writhe, her movements seeming both protest and plea. He decided to heed the latter. The last ninety-six hours had been as much a hell for her, he'd bet solid money on it. She needed this last connection as badly as he did.

"Oh," she stammered again. "Ahhh!" She yelped as he found the line of her panties. He tilted his face and caught her bottom lip with his teeth.

"Sssshhh, honey." He grinned, certain he could taste her rising lust on her mouth. "Unless you *want* everyone to know what I'm doing to you in here? What I'm about to do?"

"No!" She retorted it as her hips bucked, just as his fingers wafted over the warmth of her pussy. "I mean *no*, Mark! You can't! We...can't...do..."

He shook his head. "*No* isn't a safe word, Rose. Neither is *can't*. Besides, you still haven't given me an answer to my question." He tugged her panties down with two jerks and then slipped a finger between her moist curls, right into the heart of her steaming, tight sex. "I've had to go and find the answer for myself. And what have I discovered? Ohhh, you *are* wet everywhere, my love. Very much so."

"Yes." It was a strangle of sound now. Her head fell back as her face betrayed what her mind wouldn't yet accept. "B-But that doesn't mean we should— *Oh!*"

Her cry came as he pulled out his finger, only to deliver a firm swat across her whole mound.

He brought his hand down harder. "One spank for making me answer my own question." He gave the command with his lips still against hers. "And another for making me seek the answer to my own question. Third and last, you'll take a hard swat for protesting your Sir when he wants to give you a fucking to remember him by."

He gave her the third blow with even more force, and she reacted with a long, needy whimper. Christ, she floored him. This woman was custom molded in heaven to be a submissive. The very tint of her skin changed, a delicious flush now illuminating her from within. He finally released her lips, though he lingered close, mingling his breaths with hers, transfixed by watching her arousal transform her.

"Now...pop quiz," he challenged. "What does a good subbie say when her discipline is done?"

She swallowed deeply and then whispered back, "Thank you, Sir."

He crushed his lips to hers. "My good little student."

To his shock, a little wince creased her features. "Yes," she said, returning the intensity of his stare now, letting him see the sorrow in hers. "Yours. Always." Tears threatened the rest. "Damn it—"

"No." He issued the retaliation from tight teeth. He released her hands to clutch the back of her head. "Stop it. Not now. Reality is still thirty-thousand feet below us. You won't think about that. You'll focus on this, on us, on remembering every second of this. Do you understand?" He gripped her harder when all he received was a frantic nod. "I don't think I heard that, pet."

"Yes." With the admission came the heavy-lidded gaze and parted lips that told him she meant it, that she was slowly dipping into the misty, magical mental state to which he loved taking her the most. "Yes, Sir."

He returned a rough hum of approval, and she melted even more in his arms. He felt his mind career with hers, spiraling higher into that incredible place where he was full, uninhibited Dom. *Her* Dom. God, how he loved her for this. The power filled him, pumping into his veins and muscles, making him grip her harder, causing her to writhe and tremble in delicious little waves.

Her movement made her underwear slip farther down, loosening at her knees and then plummeting to her ankles. "Take them off the rest of the way," Mark ordered. "Then give them to me."

He watched her bend in compliance, hissing as her cheek slid along his crotch, especially when she stopped and nipped at the pounding ridge there. With a rush of impatience, he pulled her up. He yanked the panties from her grip, loving the heat in her stare as he lifted them to his nose.

"Ambrosia." He breathed deeply, the scent of her sex hitting him like an exotic drug. She let out a jagged sigh. "You smell like passion and fire, pet. Like sweet, exquisite surrender. And completely like *mine*."

She gasped into his mouth as he tossed the panties into the sink and then captured her lips again. This time he kissed her with brutal force, stabbing his tongue into the depths of her throat, letting her know exactly what he planned to do next. She was a mini earthquake in his arms when he set her free, her lips parted, her eyes closed, her nostrils flared. "Yes," he hissed. "Yes, pet. Give it all to me!"

The plane's intercom dinged, and one of the attendants announced they'd be descending for Chicago soon.

"Shit!" Rose sobbed.

"You're not going anywhere." As if concurring, his dick all but tore its way free from the jeans he'd worn for "comfort." He ripped at the button and then the fly, clenching the moan back into his throat as his hard, heavy length sprang free. Without wasting time, he jammed her skirt back up with both hands. He grunted with pleasure as his touch met the generous curves of her thighs, the pulsing heat of her pussy. Swiping fingers through the folds beneath her pubic hair, he found her soaked and swollen. She let out an awkward snort of her own, obviously muting her own lusty cry, and it had to be the sexiest damn thing he'd ever heard.

"Touch me too," he said into her ear. "Put your hand around me. Guide my cock into your cunt, pet."

Her fingers were heaven. They dragged at his base first, exploring him, one of her fingers tracing the thick vein at the underside. When he encouraged her with a hard gasp, she wrapped and stroked until she got to his hood, where his throbbing head was already covered in generous pre-come.

"You're wet too."

"It means I can't wait to be inside you." He clenched his jaw to keep himself from exploding in her hand. "Honey, I didn't bring a condom. Has there been anyone for you since Owen?"

She gave a wry smile and shook her head. "You don't even have to worry about him, Sir."

He popped a wide stare. "So you were a virgin when we..."

"No, no." Her cheeks bloomed. "But let's say it'd been a while before that."

"Oh, Rosalind." He kissed her fast to ensure her his chastising tone wasn't meant for her. She got the point, gripping his cock harder, giving him so much of herself even down to the magic of her fingertips. "There's been no one for me since Heather," he told her, letting her press his head past her curls, between her folds. "There'll be no one after you."

Her face crumpled. Soft tears fell from her passion-filled gaze. "I love you, Sir. That won't change. That'll never change!"

"And I love you, pet."

And then he was gone. Devoured by her body. Consumed by her heat. Drowned in her love.

As soon as he was buried in her core, Rose wrapped her arms around his neck. He hiked both her thighs around his waist, using the angle to get even deeper, to take them both even higher. He heard the flight crew bustling around on the other side of the door, oblivious to the No-Fires code he and Rose were blatantly violating in this little compartment. He had to grind their pace instead of pound it, increasing the friction to her clit more than he ever had before. Within minutes she started to gasp and shudder, her fingernails digging into his scalp and nape, wordlessly begging him for release. No, Mark vowed. Not yet. Not without one last precious gift of submission from her.

He turned his mouth against her ear and released a deep

growl. "Beg me for it. Tell me what you need."

She burrowed her face into his neck and whispered her reply. "Please let me come, Master. I need to come for you."

Master.

A joyous smile ignited him with the sound of it. So much better than *Senator.*

"Yes, pet. Master says you can come."

Her orgasm hit two seconds later. It turned her pussy into a vise around him, milking his raging fireball of a release. He dug his hands into her ass as he pumped his seed into her, as an equally amazing thought crossed his mind. If they got lucky, he'd just planted a baby inside her too. And if they had to move to goddamn Timbuktu to raise the child, he'd throw on a loincloth and be the happiest bastard on the globe for it.

But right now they were headed for Chicago. The attendant shattered their reverie with her pestering *ding* again, directing everyone on board to get back into their seats and prepare for the landing at O'Hare. With a quiet curse, he set Rose down and helped her get cleaned up. When she reached for her underwear, however, he shook his head.

"I'm keeping these. Last-time souvenir." He jammed them into his pocket.

She giggled and shook her head as he unlocked the door, acting as recon for their escape from the bathroom. He nodded to her and then grabbed her hand and led her out. But when they got back into the cabin, he tugged her into the seat next to his. If only for a few minutes more, she still belonged at his side. And right now, he didn't give a flying fuck who saw that or who knew.

And that included his own daughter.

Who looked up and flashed a huge grin at them both.

He scooped Rose's hand into his as she caught Dasha's look too. His little submissive blinked like she'd just been shown a crazy magic trick, but the moment was over as fast as it occurred. Dasha was now busy giggling at some joke between Pennington and Moridian as the three of them buckled in. Mark shook his head and chuckled. The way those two men fawned over her was, from his point of view, sharpened at times on a stone of solid strange, but he couldn't deny that Dasha had never glowed more in her life. If the pair wanted to keep dueling for her love like a couple of dandies in heat, then so be it. After all, especially now, he was the last one to throw stones at *anyone's* unconventional courting methods.

He turned his attention back to the woman who proved those words more true than anyone. He didn't look out the window, even as they landed and taxied to the gate. The minutes screamed by, and he wished that maybe, just maybe, if he kept staring at her and gripping her, something would change. Fate would really throw him the big brass fucking ring. She'd look at him and tell him Timbuktu didn't sound like a bad idea. Better yet, she'd grin and say, "Shane who?" Best of all, she'd get up out of that seat, keeping her fingers curled in his, and say with a smile, "Please take me home, Master."

The fantasy—and the hope—faded from his heart as she slipped her hand from his.

He craved one last glance, one final gaze, but her face was already ducked away. Her shoulders were hunched, even as she stood and jerked through the motions of reorganizing things in her bag.

It was unavoidable. He reached out again, clamping her elbow. "Rose."

She pressed her fingers atop his. "Be happy, okay?" she

whispered. "I just want you to be happy."

"Goddamn it!" He cleared his throat and sucked in a breath. "*You* make me happy!"

He forced himself into silence as she fell back into her seat, curling in on herself. If he forced this issue, if he continued beating her with all of it, then he was just as much a selfish dickwad as her brother. He had to respect what she'd decided, no matter how much this felt like a limb amputation, Civil War-style. No morphine. No clean tools. No mercy.

No sanity left at the end.

"All right," he finally muttered. "All right."

He refused to say goodbye. Because despite everything, even now, he was still a tenacious, optimistic, fuck-the-odds fool.

CHAPTER EIGHTEEN

Rose's hands, clutched in her lap, were drenched with tears by the time she raised her head again. Her motive for the move was purely selfish. She needed one last look. Even if she could only gaze at his proud, broad back, she'd have one last drop of his presence to last her until the heartache set in and—

Fear gashed into her. He'd already gotten off the plane. Just about everyone else had too. How long had she been sitting here?

Worst of all, how far had he gotten during those wasted minutes?

"Shit."

She surged to her feet, grabbing her purse and racing up the plane's center aisle. The flight attendant yelled after her, protesting about the laptop and carry-on she'd left behind, but she barely heard through the ringing in her ears. She needed to see him again. She needed to—

"Oh, God." She stopped short, feet feeling like concrete blocks. Her words were more sobs than syllables, springing from an understanding that had come so damn late.

Too damn late.

She'd slept through the alarm, hadn't she? She now had the answer, but destiny had rescinded its offer.

"I don't need to *see* him. I need to be with him. I need *him.*"

"And he needs you, Rose."

She gasped. The words had come from a face resembling

his. Strong lips, set with conviction. Eyes glowing with tawny warmth—and deep understanding.

"D-Dasha," she stammered. "I'm so confused!"

The young woman laughed. "Yeah. Love will do that to you."

She winced. "Shit. So you know?"

Dasha took her hands. "Rose, he's my *dad*. I've known since about thirty seconds after you walked into the classroom last week." Her grip tightened. "And I think it's wonderful. And there are *a lot* of other people who will agree with me."

Joy and love dueled against disbelief and doubt in her heart. "Oh, hell. We're not a magazine-cover couple. I've got quirks. A lot of them."

She'd hardly gotten that out when Dasha let out a long, loud giggle. She finished it by pulling her into a fierce hug. "Girlfriend, you don't know the half of my quirks."

Rose still shook her head. "What do I do?"

Dasha stepped closer. When her stare locked with Rose's this time, it was full of undeniable intent. "You go make my dad happy, Rose. *Please* make him happy. It's been so long for him, and it's all I want for him."

She looked at Dasha, at the conviction and confidence in her eyes, and this time, she knew what fate had done for her. Perhaps just this once, the clock was getting turned back. Here it was. The second chance. The extension on the alarm. Did she have the courage to bound out of bed this time? Did she have the guts to wake up, to open up, to love as her body, soul, and heart yearned to?

Dasha didn't give her any grace period to change her mind. The young woman was already on her cell and punching in a speed dial number.

"Dad? Where are you? Well, stop right there. You... ummm...forgot something." She punched the line shut. "VIP holding area for the limos, end of the tarmac. Go get him, Rose. Now!"

★ ★ ★

She saw him even through her tears.

The experience was better and worse than she expected.

All the fears came rushing back and more. What the hell was she doing? How on earth did her feet keep carrying her forward when they felt made of terror and ice? But then he pivoted just a little, and she beheld his beautiful, noble profile again. He took her breath away even from forty yards away. The longing came then, pulling her toward him like a lifeline. And then the desire, so magnificent, blowing her from behind like a sweet sea wind.

And the love, consuming her everywhere. A miracle. A gift.

She kept going. He kept her going. She was almost there—

She was brought up short by a very large arm. It was encased in a very black suit, which happened to be the same color as the guy's sunglasses, crew cut, and grimace.

"Uh, hi." She tried a friendly smile. Mr. Personality didn't flinch. "I'd like to speak with Senator Moore, please."

The guy's head tilted, scanning her fast. Her first inclination was to dive straight for insecurity again. But damn it, she'd overcome way too much—namely, her own shitty psyche—to let *this* goon stop her from getting to her Master.

"Special security holding area, ma'am." The guy's monotone was so cliché he must've rehearsed it. "We're sorry, but nobody in or out except the assigned VIPs and immediate family or staff."

She took a deep breath. Then looked him in the glasses, which she hoped led to his eyes, and set her chin. "I'm his fiancée."

The agent cocked his head. He was either part Collie or he didn't believe her.

"Fine, then. I might be carrying his baby. *Immediate* enough for you?"

With a grunt, Mr. Tall, Dark, and Asshole finally let her through.

As she stumbled into the exclusive area, Mark turned. He strode forward, his eyes wide.

"Rose." It was a harsh grate. "Ah hell. Are *you* what Dasha was—"

"Yes, Sir."

Without another word, he opened his arms. She didn't remember the steps she took to get to him. Perhaps she flew. It would've made sense, with how high her heart soared. His chest was solid and warm as he crushed her close, desperately kissing her neck, her cheeks, her lips.

"My love." She dampened his shirt with her tears. "My Sir. I needed—"

"I know. It's okay. And I'm here, pet. You know I'll always be here for you."

"As I'll always be here for you."

That's when he started to get it. His breath caught. He shifted his hold, tilting her face back so he could probe her with his dark-gold gaze. "What are you saying, Rose?"

"I'm saying...I've been stupid. And you're right. This is a gift. Our gift. And I want to fight for it. For you." She ran a thumb over his cheek and beard. "I don't want to listen to the past anymore. I don't want to run anymore." Her chest clutched in fear again, but she got the next words out too. "I...I'm going to reapply for a Stateside position. I can be of good use to the project right here, and I figure we can make some trips to the site together as well. You can teach me more. About all of it." When he reacted with thick silence, self-doubt immediately nicked in. "Oh shit. I mean, that's only if you still want me here?"

A harsh sound rumbled from his chest. "You'd better shut up and kiss me again, pet."

After she pressed her lips to his, a smile bloomed across them—which suddenly dipped into a confused frown. "How did you get back here? They always lock me up like a damn zoo tiger."

"Oh yeah. That." She cocked her head and grimaced sheepishly. "I sort of told them...we're engaged."

Her anxiety about his reaction got drowned by his jubilant laugh. He cut it short long enough to wrap his hand around the back of her head, crashing her lips hard to his again.

"Well," he finally said, letting her up for air. "That's one good way to get the job done."

EPILOGUE

A late-afternoon breeze stirred from the surface of Lake Michigan, cooling the September day as Rose adjusted her wedding veil. She looked around the sumptuous bedroom of Mimi Marston's Evanston mansion, which was now in chaos, and couldn't help laughing.

"What is it, sweetikins?" The gentle query came from Mimi herself, a stunning blonde dressed in a mint-green St. John sheath. Mimi was a borderline eccentric but had become one of Rose's favorite people after she and Mark made their relationship public. "Is everything all right?" the woman added.

Rose nodded. "Everything's fine. I just can't believe that last week Mark and I were in Baghdad, doing a check on the project and playing soccer in the street with a bunch of kids. Now we're, here and...I'm just..."

"It's all right, Rosalind," Mimi filled in when she broke off. "Go ahead, say it. You're deliriously, fucking happy." The woman giggled and shook her head. "Listen, sugar cake. We've all made our plays for Mark through the years—and we all knew he was being damn picky. It was just our fondest hope for him to find someone who didn't grab him by the balls, throw the wool over his eyes, and take him for a ride on the gold-digger train. We're all so glad he's found you. Make him delirious in return, and you don't have a problem here."

Her heart filled with warmth, and she gave Mimi as much

a hug as her Vera Wang gown would allow. She'd had the designer give the dress several Victorian touches, such as a classic corset bodice and a subtle little bustle, knowing they'd bring a smile to Mark's face. He'd only been specific about one aspect of her look for today, and in direct obedience, she'd had her hair styled loose and wavy over her bare shoulders.

"Thank you, Mimi. I'm going to try. And thank you for the use of the house and the lawn...and for everything. I couldn't have planned even half of this on my own."

"Awww, sweetie. This has been more fun than throwing together Amber Preston's fortieth in Atlantic City. And believe me, *that* was fun!"

Their shared laughter over that was interrupted by male footsteps on the patio outside. Dante Tieri's distinct baritone followed. "Knock, knock. Rose? You in there? I believe it's time for you to re-domesticate my best friend, darling."

"Come in, Mr. Tieri." Mimi chimed it as she dashed a quick look at herself in the vanity mirror. "All of us girls are decent...but some of us would be happy to change that status for you, gorgeous."

Dante chuckled and flashed his flawless signature smile. "Why don't we all make it to the reception first, Ms. Marston?"

"Yes, Sir." The woman's eyes dropped demurely. Rose bit back another giggle. Mimi Marston, a closet kinkster? One could never tell what lay beneath people and their shells. She just knew it felt wonderful to be out from beneath hers, set free from fear, about to be joined with the man who had made it all possible.

Dante pulled her out of her reverie, looking around the room with curiosity. "Your mother and your brother aren't here?"

Rose picked up her bouquet, a simple arrangement of burgundy and white roses. "They're seated already." She shrugged at the twinge of sadness in the man's gaze. "It's all right, really. They've both had a lot to adjust to since April. They'll either get used to it, or they won't." A little laugh sneaked in. "Maybe we should've given in to their special request of inviting Tristan Rouselle. Guess Mother would be in a better mood then."

"Really?" Dante's sarcastic snort had her doing a double take. When Rose impaled him with a questioning stare, he glanced away and muttered, "Not sure Rouselle would be coming for the company of your *mother*, darling."

The string quartet on the lawn began a new tune, bumping their volume with it. As the lush strains of Bach filled the air, the small crowd of guests rose from their seats.

It was time.

Her knees wobbled beneath her. She gripped Dante tighter with each step they took. For the first time today, true apprehension filled her. She caught sight of Mother and Shane, their faces etched in forced propriety. There were some other similar faces, from that other day when she'd expected to have a wedding ring on her finger within the hour. What if she turned the corner and the altar in front of her was empty again? What if Mark had decided she really wasn't worth his patience, his dominance, his love? What if her heart was about to endure five hundred times the damage Owen had ever dealt it?

You don't belong here. This shouldn't be happening. This is too good to be true, you know. The fairy tale is about to—

Begin.

She gazed down the aisle, and there he was. Tall. Smiling. Proud. Breathtaking.

His Marine Corps dress blues framed his form perfectly, accentuating the breadth of his shoulders and the muscles rivaling men half his age. He straightened when she turned onto the white carpet strewn with burgundy rose petals, nodding when David Pennington, his best man, leaned and murmured something to him. Standing on the other side of the gazebo was Dasha, who'd joyously agreed to be her maid of honor. They'd quickly become friends over the last few months with Dasha lending her star power to Rose's events for Iraqi children and Rose returning the favor by volunteering at the Chicago branch of the American Cancer Society.

For now, the pop star provided a soundtrack of tears as she and Mark traded their traditional vows, rings, and a searing kiss for luck that had Rose wondering how soon she could start that "luck" in their honeymoon suite at the Peninsula Hotel. Unfortunately, a little over a hundred guests wandered across the grass to wait for them beneath a twinkle-lighted canopy, now glowing even brighter as the sun dipped beyond the water.

Rose sighed and looked up at her husband as the photographer declared he was finished with their post-ceremony shots. "On to phase two?" she asked.

Mark's eyes burned with dark-gold intent. This heat was different than his intensity during the ceremony, when she'd felt like he burned each vow into her as he spoke it. "Not yet," he whispered, clutching her hand. "Come walk with me. There's something else we need to discuss."

Rose gulped. Shit. What was making him so serious? As they stopped at the edge of the lawn, now drenched in deep-orange light from the sunset, she attempted a little laugh.

"Uh, Senator Moore? You do know that prenups are usually signed *before* the wedding?"

He robbed the words from her lips by yanking her close and smashing his mouth to hers. This kiss was different than the sexy make-out smooch he'd given as her new husband. This was a possession, a raw command of her Dom. She whimpered in fierce need, letting him take whatever he needed.

"I love you so much." He growled it against her lips.

"As I love you." Rose sighed it.

He pulled up her left hand, kissing the finger that now held her goose-egg-sized wedding ring. "Rose...you know this is only half of belonging to me, right?"

She obediently dropped her lashes as soon as that distinct timbre entered his voice: the tone that told her he'd shifted completely into Dominant mode. She replied quietly, "Yes, Sir."

"Then you'll also wear this for me."

She lifted her gaze.

Then gasped.

"Oh." She ran her finger along the baguette diamonds encrusted into the shiny white leather collar. Between each jewel, the leather was embossed and then hand-painted with an exquisite burgundy rose. The choker cinched at the back with a pure gold lock. Mark held the key with gentle care, a symbol of the same way he looked after her heart every day.

"It's beautiful."

"It means forever." His voice was solemn. "Do you understand?" He tilted her face up with a finger beneath her chin. "Are you ready?"

She nodded, unable to hold back the tears anymore. They spilled and flowed as he kissed her again, locking the collar around her neck in the same motion. When he was done, his eyes filled with golden adoration.

Rose smiled and whispered the words that sang out from every depth of her soul, filling her with a joy she'd never imagined possible.

"I love you, my Sir. My Master. My Husband."

"In permanent marker?"

She laughed. Then released a sigh filled with the joy in her heart and the completion in her soul. A sigh full of the love he'd given her...and made her believe in once more.

"Yes. Oh, yes."

Continue the Suited for Sin Series with Book Three

Submit

Keep reading for an excerpt!

EXCERPT FROM *SUBMIT*

BOOK THREE IN THE SUITED FOR SIN SERIES

"Can stars really collide?"

The question came from the lips, coated with dark-red lipstick, of Dante Tieri's date for the evening. Her name was Suzanne Collier—*Suzanne*, not "Suz" or "Suzie," she was sure to tell him—and the question was actually refreshing. It was the first thing she'd said all night that didn't involve his clothes, his business, or his new condo at the Elysian, as well as the tour she clearly expected at the end of the night. In short, she was one of his usual date selections. Blonde, beautiful, young, vivacious, but close enough to his forty-three that nobody cocked a brow. The checklist went on from there, and nearly all the boxes were filled. To all who cared, he'd made an ideal selection for one of the most important Chicago events he bankrolled each year.

Which made his yawn, concealed as he reached for more champagne, *not* an encouraging thing.

"I'm not sure Elton John was thinking about cosmic physics when he wrote the song, darling." He smiled, amused at gazing into her kohl-caked eyes and facing the cloudy effects of the alcohol. Maybe she'd be more interesting after he got a few more flutes into her. "It's a great lyric, though. One of my—"

Suzanne stole the last word off his lips by smashing hers to them. It was a kiss of determination, enforced by her hand at his nape, gripping him hard. Instinct compelled him to hold her waist as she went for tongue play, though he guessed the

Taittinger had dulled his blood. His body reacted with a mild surge of warmth, nothing more. He opened a little wider, letting her explore him, groaning as she dived for his tonsils with nearly professional confidence.

He did a mental pullback. Shit. She really did kiss like a pro.

He yanked back physically too.

"Thank you," he managed to murmur. "But, umm, appearances, darling." He gazed across the room, through the forest of military dress attire, knowing damn well that none of these people cared who the hell he was or whether he humped an ostrich in front of them. "I'm sure you understand."

"Certainly." Suzanne's reply matched the smooth line she ran down his sleeve with a dark-red fingernail. "Just wanted you to have a preview for later."

He started running a list of I've-gotta-call-it-an-early-night excuses.

His effort was interrupted by a whoop from the dance floor that sliced the air as the ballad ended. The outburst was so loud, it visibly shook the banner overhead.

THANK YOU, CHICAGO VETERANS, ACTIVE DUTY, AND FAMILIES.

As the disc jockey hit the Play button on a bass-heavy dance tune, Dante joined the rest of the crowd to observe his best friend, Mark Moore, sweeping a curvy brunette off her feet. The man's grin was brilliant against his well-trimmed beard as he twirled her a couple of times and then set her down and grabbed her hand, setting a path back to where Dante sat with Suzanne.

Dante greeted the couple with a smirk he had to paste to his lips. Their giddy delight in each other was so palpable, it made his embrace with Suzanne seem a cartoon. His chest went taut. *Fuck. Just admit it, you asshole. You envy him. More than a little. It's ugly as hell, but it's the truth.*

"Well, Rose." He managed to fake his way through an easy drawl at least, addressing the gorgeous woman nestled against his friend's chest. "Marker Man doesn't raise the roof like that unless there's a damn good reason. And I have a feeling his 'damn good reason' means I'm about to lose a tremendous employee." He arched his brows at Mark. "You talked her into it after all, eh? You put a ring on her finger just two months ago, and now you want her around on a full-time basis? This is the thanks I get for footing the bill on your annual love child of a pet project?"

"Bite me, Tieri." Mark chuckled. "The marines were half my life. And didn't you just sign the contract to bankroll the Memorial Day cruise on the lake too? I think somebody just likes ogling women in uniform."

Suzanne grabbed his elbow. "I could get a uniform."

He was able to ignore her, thanks to Rose Fabian-Moore's musical laugh. "Mr. Tieri, you could turn that gift for flattery into a new business. I'm not *that* huge of a loss. You have some amazing consultants on the Baghdad project."

He grunted. "None who've cared more about getting that school rebuilt, Rose."

The classic angles of her face crunched with emotion. "Yes. I'll really miss those kids." She glanced up at Mark. "Maybe we could take just one more quick trip there, to say good—"

"No." His friend nearly snarled the word. Dante furrowed

the brows he'd just hiked at the man. He knew about Mark's intensity; hell, he shared the trait to many degrees. But he'd never seen Marker Man this ferocious. "No," Mark repeated. "And that's final. Baghdad is no place for a pregnant woman."

Shock froze him for a second. Then he surged off the stool. "What. The. Fuck? You spunky dog!" He yanked his friend into a hug. "No wonder you hollered like a teenager. Congrats, man."

"Thanks." Mark said it with heavy meaning. "That means a lot, Inferno Boy."

Though he chuckled at the nickname, Dante had to turn his gaze away again, lest Mark see what was going on in his soul. The self-honesty that had propelled him to millionaire status now turned traitor, forcing him to recognize that his envy had mutated to jealousy.

Goddamn it, there was no denying it. He craved what Mark had found. The connection. The need. Yeah, even the protective snarls. He longed for the magic his friend had been brave enough to go after with all emotional guns blasting, despite the silly social whispers that had followed. Mark and Rose shared something that drowned it all out anyhow. Their love played a symphony of its own, blasting away those small minds and their meaningless squeals of disapproval. The two of them were certainly none the worse for wear in getting deleted from half the social invitation lists in the city. To be frank, they seemed happier for it.

Hell. He could really get used to a calendar like that.

"Umm...Mr. Tieri? Are you busy?"

The shy greeting, coming from just out of his periphery, forced Dante to turn back. A female navy officer now stood there, a lieutenant if he read the stripes on her shoulder accurately, who looked ready to bolt from nervousness. He smiled out of sheer sympathy for the petite redhead. She was bracketed by two friends. A blonde, equally tiny, joined her in the squirming act. The last member of the trio, a taller brunette, stood off to the side and rolled her eyes in the universal code for *get me out of here right now*. His gaze was pulled to her. He got this reaction from a lot of people and prided himself in easing it by turning on the old-world Italian charm he'd learned so well from the source of the stuff: his grandfather. He tilted a big grin and—

It froze. *He* froze.

The halt to his gut, his chest, and his rational thinking happened sometime just after the rest of his senses fell ass over elbows into the magic of looking at her. Her sable hair was pulled back into a typical naval bun, now seeming more a goddess's knot on her head. Her dramatic brows swept over forest-deep eyes. Her mouth was a generous sweep of dark cherry, the bottom a bit fuller than the top. Her nose wasn't perfect, thank God, with a slight rounded tip that seemed made for kissing. Her strong chin perfectly finished the heart shape of her face.

His gaze dipped, taking in the rest of her. God save him, he couldn't help it. She was slim yet curved in all the right places. Her breasts looked gentle and plush, decent handfuls that were matched by the soft swell of her ass, and legs that made her government pumps look as erotic as pole-dancer stilts. Damn it, when had naval skirt suits gotten so sexy?

He told himself to shake it off. To crack some lame one-liner that would set her at ease and make her want to stay here, in his direct universe, nearly close enough to touch. Shit, just thinking of *touching* her—well, now he knew what creative visualization meant, didn't he? As well as sweet torture.

As well as complete irony.

Three minutes ago, he'd tossed a symbolic coin into the fountain of fate. He'd waved his goddamn melodramatic mental flag, declaring cravings for connection and need, possessiveness to the point of going feral about it, a lover and not just a date.

Something a lot like this.

In the back of his mind, he heard fate giggling at him. Hysterically.

This story continues in Submit Suited for Sin Book Three!

ALSO BY ANGEL PAYNE

Suited for Sin:
Sing
Sigh
Submit

The Bolt Saga:
Bolt
Ignite
Pulse
Fuse
Surge
Light

Honor Bound:
Saved
Cuffed
Seduced
Wild
Wet
Hot
Masked
Mastered
Conquered
Ruled

Secrets of Stone Series:
No Prince Charming
No More Masquerade
No Perfect Princess
No Magic Moment
No Lucky Number
No Simple Sacrifice
No Broken Bond
No White Knight
No Longer Lost
No Curtian Call

Temptation Court:
Naughty Little Gift
Pretty Perfect Toy
Bold Beautiful Love

Cimarron Series:
Into His Dark
Into His Command
Into Her Fantasies
Into His Sin

**For a full list of Angel's other titles,
visit her at AngelPayne.com**

ACKNOWLEDGMENTS

Humble, grateful hugs to Jade Barker, Kimberly Ream, Tracy Roelle, and Jodi Lucius for being my first reader cheerleaders. You all made my first steps into this a more joyful and incredible experience!

So many thanks to all the bloggers and reviewers who first loved this series. Your belief has meant so much!

Special thanks to Victoria Blue, who encouraged me to get these books back into the world again.

So many hugs of gratitude to Martha Frantz, For keeping me sane on a daily basis!

And for all of the Roses in the world...

Find your fantasy island.

Find yourself.

And never be afraid to let that freak flag fly, no matter what the world says.

ABOUT ANGEL PAYNE

USA Today bestselling romance author Angel Payne loves to focus on high-heat romance starring memorable alpha men and the women who love them. She has numerous book series to her credit, including the action-packed Bolt Saga and Honor Bound series, Secrets of Stone series (with Victoria Blue), the intertwined Cimarron and Temptation Court series, the Suited for Sin series, and the Lords of Sin historicals, as well as several standalone titles.

Angel is a native Southern Californian, leading to her love of being in the outdoors, where she often reads and writes. She still lives in Southern California with her soul-mate husband and beautiful daughter, to whom she is a proud cosplay/culture con mom. Her passions also include whisky tasting, shoe shopping, and travel.

Visit her at AngelPayne.com